The Book of Joe

Michael Carley

For Ann Marie

CONTENTS

Yet man is born to trouble

   as surely as sparks fly upward

                Job 5:7

One must feed the dying embers

for that's where the next flame grows

Though the source of the fuel you'll be burning

is not for you to know.

.

PROLOGUE

There are many reasons why international trade negotiations are conducted in secret. The nations involved represent, not only, not even primarily, and occasionally, not at all, the will of their citizens, but rather a combination of the business interests that are prominent in their regions and among their leadership, and know enough to contribute their own knowledge, expertise, and resources, financial, personal, political, and diplomatic, to the metaphorical, and sometimes, literal, table. The bargaining is interest-based, but each nation, corporation, and individual involved has a different set of interests at stake, and a different level of willingness to share those interests with the rest of the group.

There are occasions, however, when the confluence of those interests, and of the sundry and mind-numbingly detailed compromises among the players involved, results in an agreement which the majority of those players believe is in the best interests of enough of those that they represent that it will be to the benefit of most, and signatures are affixed to paper, pieces are moved on virtual chessboards, and real gains and losses are made, in the health, economic, and environmental atmosphere in which the people of the world reside.

As happens in any game of chess, pawns must be sacrificed. What is less known is that not all players know when and whether they are pawns.

CHAPTER 1

The banquet hall was filled, and the aisles were crowded, but his seat at the front gave Joe a vantage point most would envy. As his name was about to be called, he wiped his chin and waited patiently. The Peking Duck had been tasty, and he'd come to enjoy events such as these. At this point in his life, they no longer made him nervous nor excited. He was comfortable in his world. The speaker was ending his introduction, so Joe pushed away his utensils, but waited to pull out his chair. He wasn't anxious and didn't want to appear so.

"….a list of accomplishments too long to mention here, especially because I know most of you would rather hear from our honoree than myself. Not only has he built an impressive corporation, from the ground up, I would add, he has used it, and the fame and fortune that came with it, to make the world a better place for all of us. Solar Champions aren't just the biggest providers of solar panels in the western United States. They are a leader in investing in technologies that will take us into the future, not, as Joe often reminds us, saving the world, but perhaps saving our ability as a species, to continue to live on it as we do.

But it isn't just through the corporate arena that Joe has made a difference. If that were his only contribution, we likely wouldn't be here. Through the Joe and Sophia Taylor Foundation, they have found ways to not only ensure our future existence on the planet, but to make it livable and meaningful. Their contributions to rainforest protection has prevented thousands of acres of prime forest from being harvested. Their education initiatives are so numerous, well, I'll not bore you, but they're impressive. And right here in the Bay Area, Joe and Sophia have taken on the biggest challenges, homelessness, not only through generous donations— one of which resulted in the largest shelter in the state, dedicated last year—but also to research and development of new housing, both making lives better on a daily basis and finding ways to reduce the problem at its core.

There is much more that could be said, but I will end it here. In short, Joe is accomplishing what many of us have often thought impossible. He is doing well and doing good at the same time. As his own fortunes have improved, he has paid it forward in ways that put many of us to shame. Without further ado, I introduce you to Joseph Taylor—we all know him as Joe—OUR Humanitarian of the Year!"

Joe walked up the steps to the dais, and as the speaker reached out his hand for a shake, pulled him in for a close hug before stepping up to the lectern. He had to wait several moments before beginning his speech as the ovation had not subsided. Finally, he raised his hand and gestured amiably for the audience to take their seats. The applause increased momentarily before obedience took hold, with each member of the crowd reluctantly sitting, Sophia being last among them, her face aglow. Joe nodded in her direction before speaking.

Thank you, thank you all so much. An award like this, it feels...well, hopefully, just a bit premature. You see, I thought we were just getting started with our work. Surely, others are more worthy.

Honestly, I wanted to turn this down. I like doing, not speechifying. I'd rather let the work speak for itself. But, the Bay Area Inter-agency Forum and its hardworking leaders, well, they can be very persuasive. They said that perhaps there is something that could be learned from what we have done—done so far, I would remind you, because we're nearer the beginning than the end, I do hope—that might lead to better corporate citizenship among the leaders of tomorrow.

I don't know about that myself, but for whatever it might be worth, I will try to share a bit about our philosophy of service and leadership.

When I started this company, I had little more than an idea for a type of solar panels that would improve efficiency. We've had a few other innovations in our time, but I don't claim to be the next Edison or Tesla. We thought bringing these to market would make money, yes, but it would also help people. It would save them power—and thus money—and it would reduce our dependence on fossil fuels. So, we found some investors, people who believed in us and in our ideas, and we managed to get some seeds planted.

Now, investors are in it for one thing: to make a profit. I was in it for one thing: to make a difference.

(Cheers from the audience; Joe holds up his hand.)

No, that doesn't make me noble or anything. For the record, I'm not allergic to profit. I like money as much as the next guy. I've been lucky enough so far that I've made quite a lot of it. I say that, not out of vanity (I hope), but from the perspective of someone who cares about what he does. My parents taught me some simple lessons: dream big, but not just for yourself. Make a difference for someone else in the world, whether that is a homeless person on the street, a homeowner looking to save some money, or the human species.

I'm sounding grandiose, so let me break it down for you. There's a philosophy we try to live by, both in our corporation, and in our household. Every decision we make has a group of stakeholders. Now, in most corporations, they will tell you that the only stakeholder that matters is the investor. Profit at all costs. We disagree.

(A few claps from the audience.)

Investors are an important stakeholder; we wouldn't be in business without them. But there are others. Workers are one. Every employee in our organization matters. Most organizations outsource their production. I'm proud to say that our panels are made right here in the USA. (audience cheers).

Let's be clear about that. We're not nationalists and there is nothing wrong with hiring where you can get the best bang for the buck. We employ American workers, not because Americans are better and foreign workers inferior, but because we believe in adhering to the highest possible standards of employee treatment and safety and we can control that more effectively by keeping it local. We've never had a union at SC (a brief whoop from the audience, but a sharp look from Joe silences the room), but it's not because we're opposed to them. Instead, the employees have representation on our board, a voice in the room.

Another stakeholder is the community. Defining community is a tricky thing. At one level, it is the local community in which we are headquartered. We certainly value the community here in Silicon Valley, just look at the housing prices.

(laughs from the audience, along with a few groans.)

For us, valuing the local community means making it a better place to live. That's not just a slogan; for us, it's a question we ask daily. How can we make life better, for our employees and for everyone who lives here? There are a few obvious examples, like city parks, which we've helped fund in several of the cities and towns surrounding our complex. The commute can be a bit of a hassle, so we allow anyone whose job doesn't require being at headquarters to work from home as much as possible. It doesn't just make their lives better; it reduces traffic for everyone. We contribute to our local school districts, not just free solar technology, but housing vouchers so they can recruit and retain good teachers and support staff, from the principal right down to the custodian.

As we've grown as a company, community doesn't just mean local. It's national, international. We can't do everything for everyone in the world—yet—but we do what we can, where we can.

There is a question we sometimes debate as to whether the natural world is part of that community, or another stakeholder in itself. In a practical sense, it doesn't matter. Our environment is important either way, and treating it as a stakeholder matters. The big difference is that nature doesn't have a voice at the table, or perhaps it does, but we have to learn to listen. The voice isn't automatic. We have to grant it. Caring for our world is important because, cliché as it may sound, it's the only one we've got.

You might think creating a product that helps reduce our dependence on fossil fuels would itself serve as an act of service to the environment, but we don't view it that way. First, while we believe our products are hugely beneficial, we cannot deny, as some of our competitors are prone to do, that there are negative impacts to any form of energy generation, including solar. The materials involved require resource extraction and to have the kind of impact we hope for on energy use, means that impact will be significant. So, we mitigate it where we can.

Again, some companies would just do the popular thing, you know the term, carbon offsets. They figure you can plant a few trees and everything is good. What they don't tell you is that the trees they plant are often not the right ones for the area. You can do a lot of damage by pushing non-native species into an area where they don't belong. I can tell you, we haven't planted many trees.

The thing is, there are places in this world where there are trees and they're under threat. Instead of planting more, we work with the people, in the Amazon and elsewhere where the rainforests are disappearing at an alarming rate, to protect the land. This is a lesson we learned from Jane Goodall. In her work protecting chimpanzee habitat, she didn't just push for poaching bans. She learned that would be ineffective because the poachers weren't the enemy, as much as one might have thought so. Desperate people are going to do desperate things. She worked with the local populations who might be prone to poaching and in doing so, she was able to protect both the humans and the chimps. We did the same. The farmers near the Amazon aren't the enemy.

They are people trying to make a living however they can. While setting aside acreage for protection, we worked with them, not against them, helping them find sustainable methods that protected the remaining forest and their livelihoods simultaneously.

We used this philosophy here in the US as well. You might remember, a few years back, there was a little kerfuffle up north between the logging companies and some activists trying to preserve the trees. In a moment of hopefully uncharacteristic hubris, I offered to serve as mediator between the sides. Now, our love for the environment had us at some level on the side of the trees, but at heart, as I explained to both sides, I remain a capitalist. So, I thought I could understand each perspective.

As it turned out, the facts of the situation made things incredibly complex. Emotions were running high. But one thing we capitalists understand is incentives. Another is markets. It seems that if those who owned the forests— these were private lands—don't cut down those trees, the market forces involved encourage others to do so. Prices go up and just because one person doesn't cut down a tree doesn't mean someone else won't. It will just be a different tree.

So, we bought the forest.

(Cheers)

Not just me, of course. But we got a group of people together, not just activists, but land conservationists, open-space advocates, and people with resources, including (gasp!) some venture capitalists. Perhaps they needed to assuage their consciences.

(laughter.)

Our work wasn't done. Remember those loggers? They still needed work. Daily tasks to maintain their dignity and sense of worth, and to put food on the table. We put the land in a trust, to be managed in perpetuity and got some of those former forestry workers to manage it. For the others, we set up funds for retraining so they could find other jobs to support their families. Most of the former workers are happy—we actually surveyed them—but not all. After all, maintaining a forest and managing it for those who want to use it responsibly is easier work than cutting down trees. Those who aren't happy, well, maybe they just loved cutting trees, or maybe they can't be made happy. One thing we've learned is we can't control everything.

There are still those market forces to contend with. We're still working on that. Some people love redwood fencing and redwood decks, but that's changing. There are new materials being created every day, some of them incredibly beautiful and easy to work with, and nearly all are more environmentally friendly than chopping down the oldest and biggest living things on the planet.

I grew up a couple hundred miles from here, in a town called Tulare, not far from the Giant Sequoia groves. They're related to the redwoods, but not the same trees. Both are beautiful in their own ways. And both need to be preserved.

I know what some of you are thinking. Billionaire privilege. It's true after all. I don't ask for any plaudits for buying a forest. We did the right thing, and it was in our capacity to do so. Not everyone has the resources we have. We each must do our part. If what I can do is more than what someone else can, it is because I've been gifted so much in this life that I have the capacity to give back.

That is, perhaps, another point I'd like to get across to you tonight. Each time we've done something for the public good, whether it is one of our educational initiatives, buying land for open space, or building a homeless shelter, the returns have come back to us. I don't just mean metaphorical or feel-good for doing a public service. I mean market expansion and stock gains.

(A smattering of applause echoes around the room.)

I don't know if it's fate or what and it is rarely a one-for-one proposition. But our business has never been better, and I am convinced that our work for the community—very broadly defined—is a part of the reason for that.

I try to live a humble life. It's why I protested coming here today. But—and at the risk of sounding trite—I am blessed. She doesn't like the spotlight, but I'd like to mention my wife, Sophia. (A spotlight finds her in the audience, and she gives a small wave.) She and our son are the lights of my life. That's him now, asleep in her arms. We thought about getting a babysitter, but we like the little guy and want to spend as much time with him as we can. He goes back to preschool on Monday.

I have it on good authority—Sophia's, in fact—that there may be a second child in our lives very soon. (Polite, happy applause.) So, when I say I am blessed, you can believe I know whereof I speak. Sophia coordinates events for the foundation; she's the one you see behind the scenes whose name you rarely get to know, but whose work makes everything else possible.

My point here today is that Sophia and I—and our child, soon to be children—we have a good life. Yes, I have stock options, enough to last us a thousand lifetimes. But, I can't eat those. We have a nice life here. We have a beautiful house. We could afford a bigger one, but I've never seen the point of having 35 rooms when seven will do. The little guy you see there will probably go to public school, but we could afford a private one if we wanted to. We have nice cars and everything we need. Yes, we're rich, I suppose, but I don't like to think about it that way. I can't think of anything else I'd like to do with all this money when there are people suffering nearby and problems to solve everywhere. I'm a billionaire, I guess, at least, that's what they tell me, I've never bothered to count. But I don't worry about moving up that list of billionaires and doing the things other billionaires do. I want to serve.

As we continue to serve, our business continues to grow. I don't need to be any wealthier, but tomorrow, I probably will be.

I've spoken longer than I intended, but I guess the point I'm circling around to is the one that was made earlier tonight as part of that lovely introduction. It is possible to both do good and do well. I am living proof of that. I want to tell you all tonight that you can, and should, reject wholesale the idea that we must make a choice between maximizing profits and serving the world. We should reject this choice because it is a false one. You can make a very good living doing the right thing. If you make the right choices, keep your eye on the goal, you'll find that doing good and doing well end up being the same thing.

At least, that's what I've found to be true so far. Thank you.

The applause was raucous as Joe put down the microphone, shook hands with the emcee, and made his way down the steps from the dais. He walked over to Sophia and found her eyes beaming as she stood along with the crowd in an extended ovation. He leaned in for a hug and she whispered, "You did good." Joe nodded, kissed his son on the cheek, and took his seat for the remainder of the evening's program.

As the event came to a close, several of the region's leading people of business approached. Most simply wanted to congratulate Joe on the award, some asked about his business or his activism, either to learn or to make themselves appear interesting. Joe answered patiently either way. The esteem with which he was regarded in the community, local and national, was genuine and well-earned.

A few were jealous and peered at him from the corners of the room, but Joe didn't notice, or seemed not to. At last, it was time to make their way out. Joe and Sophia found their car in the honored guest spot in the parking lot. Sophia placed the sleeping toddler in his car seat and Joe helped to buckle him in firmly. As they drove away, toward their handsome and humble home on the outskirts of Morgan Hill, they knew that life for them was safe and prosperous.

Joe turned their car into the secluded neighborhood, past the tall, green hedges that characterized the border of their property, and rolled quietly into the driveway, prepared for a weekend of rest and enjoyment.

CHAPTER 2

Mondays were always busy, but Joe thrived on it. From small crises to breakthroughs, he was energized by continual engagement, the solving of problems and the belief that each step taken was one toward progress.

The first hour or so had consisted of leftover congratulations and plaudits from the previous weekend's events, including some mild joshing. Executives and team members who couldn't make the shindig itself stopped by Joe's windowed office to give a kind word or to ask to see the shiny award, a request for which he disappointed them as the trophy was already tucked away in a box at home. He'd received a few awards over the years and felt that displaying them sent the wrong message. Focus on the work, not the rewards, he thought, and preached, to his team, and anyone who would listen.

The first real interruption came when Zaida Choksi, the company Chief Financial Officer, stopped by, knocked twice, and entered without waiting for the invitation they both knew was unnecessary. Zaida had only been with the company two years, but had moved up the ranks quickly. "You checked the news yet?" she asked casually.

"No, just the usual stuff. Wasn't expecting much of anything relevant to us this morning. Why, were you?"

"There are rumors out of the trade talks. May be a breakthrough."

"You know as well as I do not to take rumors seriously. The likelihood that they're accurate is less than fifty-fifty."

"I don't take them all that seriously, but the markets do. My job is different from yours, remember? I have to pay attention not just to what's happening, but what people think is happening. Because either could affect our bottom line."

"Never has before."

"Always a first time. That's why you pay me the medium bucks." Zaida's voice trailed off as she left the room; she always liked leaving on a high note. She said it helped people remember her.

Just as she was leaving, Angel, Joe's longtime assistant, knocked on the window, entering with a phone in her hand. "You check the news yet?"

"Why is everyone asking me this?"

"Sorry to spoil your Monday. Just thought you might like to know, there's a fire at the Armstrong Grove."

"Our grove? The one we got going up north with the foundation?"

"Yep, that one." She reached over and with a few keystrokes on his laptop, got the page up. Cal Fire was showing video from earlier in the day, along with announcements from a talking head.

> ...zero percent containment, though I would remind you, we're at a very early stage, still learning what is going on. We're not sure how much damage this could wreak. And, again, we're talking about private land, so our responsibility is a bit different...

"So, you're the Angel of darkness today, I see. How bad is this?"

"You know almost as much as I do. Just pulling you into the loop."

"Appreciated. Please keep up and let me know if it gets bad."

"In my copious spare time?"

"On your work time, for which you are moderately handsomely

rewarded."

"Mmm hmm."

The phone rang just as she was walking out the door.

It was Sophia. "Hi Hon.' What's up?"

"Well, I dropped off your son at day care and by the time I got home, they were already calling. He's throwing up. I'm on my way back."

"So, a little vomit and now, he's *my* son?"

"Yep. That's how it works."

"Sorry, I know you had things to do today."

"Best laid plans. Anyway, just wanted to let you know."

"OK, give the little guy a kiss for me. And keep me updated."

The next knock on the door was tentative. It was Zaida's secretary, who didn't come down this far often. "Excuse me."

"Yes."

"Ms. Choksi asked if you can join her in the conference room with the other senior leaders."

"What's going on?"

"I don't know, just seemed serious."

"On my way."

Stepping out the door, his adrenaline was beginning to flow. "Angel, walk with me, you look like you have something to say. Tell me it's good news."

"Afraid not. Just wanted to give you an update. Cal Fire says it's up to five hundred acres. No containment yet and they say it will get worse before it gets better."

"Are they protecting the redwoods like they did the Sequoias in the parks?"

"Apparently not. Some kind of jurisdictional issue. They don't have the same mandate or something."

"Mandate?"

"It's private land. We're responsible."

"Yes, but not for wildfires."

"They put out fires. We're supposed to protect the forest."

"Okay." Joe paused for a moment. "How do we do that?"

"For the moment, we can't get in, so it's something of a moot point." They were just reaching the conference room, but Angel put her hand on the door. "Joe, there's more."

"Tell me."

"Three of our workers are dead."

"The guys we hired? The former loggers we put to work managing things? What happened?"

"I don't have the details, but it sounds like they got caught behind the line before the firefighters arrived. It's part of why it took so long for them to get started on the fire itself. They had to rescue our guys first."

Inside the conference room, Zaida was waving. Whatever they needed him for, it was urgent.

Still, Joe paused a moment, took a breath, and mumbled a quick prayer before taking Angel by both hands. "Keep monitoring. And when you get back to your desk, please get me the contact information for the families of those three employees. I'll call them after this meeting."

"Will do boss."

Joe stepped into the conference room to find most of his senior staff shouting at one another. He walked to the front of the room where the financial talking heads were doing their thing on CNBC. He picked up the remote, muted the television, and raised his hand for silence. After a couple of moments, he got it.

"Who wants to tell me what's going on?"

Everyone did, apparently.

"News out of the trade talks."

"It's all bad."

"China will undercut us."

"I don't know what we're going to do."

"Stock is tanking."

That caught Joe's attention. "Oh, come on. Our stock has been going up from the day we issued our IPO. We've split three times in the past four years and never had more than a ten percent drop in a day or any drop that lasted longer than a week or two. How bad could it be?"

"Bad," came the chorus from around the room.

"What was the stock at yesterday? Thirty-something?"

"Thirty-four. Almost thirty-five."

"Thirty-four point five nine." The precise number came from Zaida, just to Joe's right. She had been quiet through most of the yelling, allowing the more frantic voices to play themselves out.

"OK, walk me through it. What's happened?"

Zaida did so, methodically, shushing the others with a look. "Nothing is confirmed yet, but as we discussed earlier, rumors prompt action, especially among our institutional investors." She looked over to one of her colleagues on the other side of the table, apparently reemphasizing a point she'd been making earlier. Forbes had an article this morning, citing three sources at the trade talks."

"Anonymously citing…." came a voice from down the table.

"A point which matters not one whit to investors," Zaida said, her patience wearing.

"What are the rumors?"

"Supposedly, there are several tradeoffs being proposed in the talks. The article was quite lengthy, but one, and it has been confirmed, supposedly from different sources, by Bloomberg, is that the tariffs on Chinese solar panels are being done away with."

"That's all? We can compete with anyone. Bring it on."

"Joe, you don't seem to understand."

"I believe in our products. Don't you?" There were affirming voices around the room.

Zaida stood. "We all believe in our products. That's not the point. They'll undercut us."

"We have a better quality product. Our materials have a lower environmental impact than theirs, or anyone else's, for that matter. Consumers know this."

"Consumers care about their pocketbooks more than anything. The difference in quality is marginal and they're not reading the charts showing savings amortized over twenty years. And American consumers know little about the relative environmental impact of various manufacturing processes, and they care even less."

"That sounds pretty cynical. We..."

"Sir, the markets are quite cynical. Consumers care about price, first, last, and always. And investors..."

"Investors know a long-term..."

"Sir, American investors don't think long-term much at all. They want performance, today."

"So, you think we'll take a hit. So what? We'll bounce back. You'll see."

"We're already taking a hit."

"How bad?"

"Twenty-eight," came a voice from down the table. "And dropping," came another, from the alternate side."

"At this moment," Zaida corrected, pointing at the screen. We're at twenty five point eight two. And this isn't the bottom. I guarantee it."

Joe sat down. He wasn't the panicking type, but they had his attention. Now, he needed theirs. "Ladies and gentlemen, I'd like to remind you that we started this company buck naked if you will forgive the metaphor. We had nothing but an idea. A new technology that met a need. We had no capital, and we built all of this. If, on the off chance, our stock goes all the way to zero, which it won't, we'll start again. American consumers gave us all we have and I have faith that they'll see us through."

The collective blood pressure of the room seemed to drop a few points. Even Zaida relaxed a bit, though she was still vigilant. She picked up the remote to turn the volume back up so they could hear the talking heads, but at just that moment, Angel knocked on the glass door. Joe waved her in.

"Angel Ramos Ortiz, before you say a word, you realize your surname means 'fortunate one,' don't you?"

"So you've told me."

Joe put on his gregarious face. "So, I'd like you to think very carefully about what you say next. Do you finally have some good news for us?"

"Not exactly."

"It's not about the fire again, is it?"

Zaida perked up with concern. "Fire? What fire?"

"I do have some news about the fire, but right now, you have a phone call. Sounds important."

"OK, what I'd like you to do, since everyone is here anyway, is to brief the team on the fire. Because the forest donation was run through the foundation, it's not technically company business, but I know several people here care a lot about it. And, point me to this important phone call."

Angel pointed. "My desk. Line three."

Joe stepped over to his secretary's desk and picked up the phone. "This is Joe Taylor."

"Mr. Taylor, this is Sergeant Ignacio with the California Highway Patrol. Can I confirm that your wife's name is Sophia?"

"Yes."

"She drives a red Toyota Prius? And your home address is on Good Hope Circle in Morgan Hill?"

"Yes, may I ask what this is regarding? Has something happened?"

"Mr. Taylor, I'm afraid your wife has been in a traffic accident. It seems that as she pulled out of the parking lot of the Happy Futures Academy preschool this morning, her car was hit from the side. It was a rather large SUV, the driver doing about 45 at the time."

"Is she OK? Our son, he was with her? Are they both OK?"

"Your wife and son were transported to Regional Medical Center. I have the address on Jackson, if you need it."

"I can find it. How are my wife and son?"

"I'm afraid I don't have more information to share on the extent of their injuries at this time, just that the accident was serious and you should have someone drive you to the hospital. Do you have someone, Mr. Taylor?"

"I'll get there. Thank you, Sergeant."

"You're welcome, Mr. Taylor. We will need to speak with you soon to collect more information. For now, I'm sure you'd like to get to the hospital. We'll be in touch soon."

Joe was no longer listening. He was running full tilt down the hall, his dress shoes clicking on the marble tile and his powder blue tie trailing after him in the air conditioning.

Angel had, by this time, briefed the team on the fire. Zaida sat, rapt and taking notes. Heads drooped around the conference room. For the rest of the morning, she kept coffee flowing and two screens at the head of the table, media reports of the fire on the left and the stock news on the right. By the time the markets closed, their price was down to four dollars and twenty-three cents a share and the room was empty.

CHAPTER 3

Composed and intent, Joe stepped through the doors of the Regional Medical Center emergency room waiting area. The receptionist looked up, and he quickly gave his name. Her face deadpan, she told him someone would be with him soon. Before he could sit down, the door buzzed and a young woman in purple scrubs called his name. He followed her into a small office. "The doctor will be with us shortly. I just need to collect some information."

Her name tag read "Lilah" and she moved through the room like a whirling dervish, her foot bouncing as she typed. She twirled a rubber band on the end of her pen, which she did not use to write because everything was on her computer screen. Smiling sweetly, she asked Joe for Sophia's insurance information, which he efficiently provided. Lilah tapped through several screens, then her face turned for a brief moment. "Excuse me," she said, and swished out of the room. She returned in a moment with a doctor who looked somber.

"Mr. Taylor?" the doctor asked.

"Yes."

"Come with me please."

The doctor escorted Joe into another small room, an office with three chairs. A painting on the wall read, "Hang in There," with a smiling orangutan suspended from a tree branch. He began without a preamble.

"Mr. Taylor, your wife and son were involved in a very serious accident."

"Yes, I know. I got the call a while ago. How are they?"

"I was getting to that." The doctor looked weary. Joe remembered himself and tried to relax. He had long known that his own state of mind affected others, something he usually addressed unconsciously. The doctor relaxed a bit himself. "Mr. Taylor. Your wife's injuries were fairly minor. She has a wrist fracture and some internal bleeding, which we've managed to repair. There wasn't time to call you beforehand, I'm afraid."

"It's OK. I'm sure it was necessary."

"Were you aware your wife was pregnant?"

"Was? Did she lose the baby?"

"No. I apologize for my phrasing. Your wife is still pregnant as we speak. But we are concerned. Her blood pressure is somewhat elevated and she's at some risk for placenta previa. Do you know what that is?"

"Not entirely, but I've heard of it."

"We can provide more detail if you like, but the bottom line is, if the two of you intend to continue with the pregnancy, she'll need to be on bed rest, at least for a few days."

"The pregnancy was planned. We do want to continue with it, unless there's some danger?"

"She's not completely out of the woods. We're watching for clots. We may prescribe a blood thinner, but the pregnancy limits our choices a bit. We think your wife will be OK, and with some luck and medical oversight, the baby should be as well. Hopefully, she'll be able to go home in a week or so."

"Our son. How is he?"

The doctor started to speak, but the words caught. He fell back on his training. "Mr. Taylor, I'm afraid your son didn't make it. I don't have all of the details, but the EMTs told us the impact was on his side of the car. I believe it was instantaneous, no time for pain."

There was more, but Joe didn't hear it. He stood, frozen, feeling as though he would shatter if time were to restart itself. After a few moments, he realized the doctor was still speaking. Willing back the tears, he apologized. "Doctor, does my wife know?"

"Yes, we were planning to wait for you to arrive, but she insisted on an update just a little while ago."

"May I see her?"

"Of course, but I just prescribed a sedative. Once she gets it, she'll likely be sleeping for several hours. And, she needs the rest, for more reasons than one."

"Of course. I'd still like to look in, if I may."

"Right this way."

The ER was busy, and Joe almost got lost trailing the doctor through the open floor plan, dodging nurses, orderlies, and others, busy at their work. It was nearing lunchtime, and trays were being passed to patients who were ready to be admitted, but for whom there was not yet a room prepared. Finally, they reached Sophia's room. The doctor called out a quiet, confident "knock knock", then parted the curtains and walked in, with Joe behind him.

Lilah was there, adjusting the IV. She finished injecting something into the tube and looked up. "Just administered the sedative, doctor," she said, as she twirled over to drop the needle and other accessories into the hazardous waste bin. She twirled back to the front of the bed, just to Sophia's left as Joe approached on the right side. As he knelt and took his wife's hand, Lilah continued to clean up, while the doctor stood at the foot of the bed for just a moment, then departed, the curtain divider swishing quietly as Joe began to speak.

"They told you?"

She turned; if she nodded, it was not discernable.

"I'm so sorry,"

"I wish it had been me."

"Honey, no." Joe shifted backward on his heels. He realized he'd been clutching her hand and released the grip, their connection severed. "We'll get through this," he told her, trying to feign a confidence he lacked.

"No."

Joe leaned forward on his haunches, temple to temple with his wife, mingling their tears. He said nothing for a moment, but finally tried. "We'll get through this…someh…"

"No," she said again. "I wish I had died instead of him. I want to die now."

She released his hand and though there was no evidence the sedative had yet kicked in, she turned to her side, away from her husband, and said no more.

Joe was stunned, uncharacteristically unsure how to react. He began to stand, but paused halfway up.

At that moment, two things happened. A food service worker parted the curtain and stepped over toward Sophia's bed, a tray containing a bowl of soup in his hand. Simultaneously, Lilah twirled for the last time, her duties for Sophia concluded, and prepared to leave. As she stepped away from the bed, her dangling blood pressure cuff caught the IV pole, twirling it with her as she collided with the cafeteria delivery. As Joe turned to see what the commotion was, he was hit in the back with a full, steaming bowl of French onion soup, followed immediately by the IV pole, which slammed down, its hooks impaling themselves directly into his back. Lilah and the cafeteria worker both backed out of the curtained area in shock.

After they had him sedated, it was several minutes before the doctors and nurses were able to get the sound of Joe's screams out of their heads.

CHAPTER 4

When his friends entered the room, Joe didn't look peaceful. Lying on his stomach to prevent further injury to his back, his face was puffy and distorted. They pretended not to notice.

They had met before, though there had been little interaction among them as their roles in Joe's life branched in different directions, connecting only occasionally. Elleanor Meier, more generally known as Pastor Ellie, led the congregation to which Joe and Sophia belonged. Offering support and spiritual guidance to patients in the hospital was par for the course. Having received a call from the hospital chaplain, she'd been on her way to be with Sophia when she learned Joe was injured.

William Thomas hadn't been called William by anyone since fifth grade, when one of his teachers insisted on that formality. He and Joe had met that same year and to Joe and everyone else, he was Billy. They played together on the basketball team and in the school band, with Billy playing trombone alongside Joe's saxophone. Billy now served on the board of the Joe and Sophia Taylor Foundation, directing its local arts initiatives.

Zaida Choksi had made it to the hospital as soon as she could, energized rather than exhausted by her long, disastrous day as the company's fortunes seemed to have gone up in both figurative and literal smoke. She continued keeping up with happenings on the drive over and via text on her way up the elevator. But though the messages kept coming in, her phone was silenced, as were those of the others. Each knew the protocol.

They hardly recognized their comrade, with his injuries, bandages, and positioning, but they were here to pay their respects. After Ellie led them in a few moments of quiet prayer, they sat silently. They remained by his side through the evening and into the night, seven hours straight, waiting for direction from the man, they had, in various ways, come to see as their leader.

CHAPTER 5

Ellie was the last remaining, the one still present when Joe awoke. It was she who disturbed him, returning from a trip to the cafeteria with her breakfast cradled in her left hand, her purse in her right. Entering his room, she unthinkingly switched on the light so she could make her way back to the chair beside the bed.

"Achhh…" Joe was still facing the floor, his voice echoing from every corner of the room, though muffled by his sheets. "Turn…off!"

Ellie complied, muttering an apology before resorting to the placid cheerfulness that her pastoral training and experience had taught her. "I'm glad to see you awake and feeling better."

"Not better."

"I'll settle for one out of two then." Ellie was happy she had her booklight with her. It had served her well in the darkness, and when

Joe slept again, would do so for however long she stayed. "I'll leave the light off until you're ready for it."

"I don't think I'll ever be ready."

"That's understandable. You've been through a lot in the past twenty-four hours. Rest up. There's no need to tackle the world's problems, or your own, for some time now."

"I don't think I'll be tackling either again. There's no point."

"Joe, you're talking to the wrong person when you say that. Faith is my business."

"I'm all out of faith."

Ellie said nothing, but she put her hand over his. "That's all right for now. Today, I'll have enough faith for the both of us."

Joe pulled his hand away, even that small movement adding to his pain, which only fueled his rising anger. He turned, for the first time and looked at his pastor, a fire in his eyes of a different quality than the simmering passion that had so often fueled his contributions to the congregation. There was a bitterness in those eyes that gave her pause, if only momentarily. But his words, though coldly uttered, were few, "You heard." It was a statement far more than a question.

"Yes, they told me."

"Then tell the doctor to bring me something to knock me out."

"Joe, I know you're in pain---"

"You know nothing."

"You're right. I can only imagine."

"No, you can't."

"Joe." Here, she paused. Rarely was she at a loss for words, even when her parishioners faced circumstances that were unfathomable. "I'm sure you're right; I can't imagine. But in circumstances like these, I always turn to my faith. It hasn't let me down yet."

"I don't have that much faith. I don't think I ever did. I'm not sure anyone could."

"Trust in God."

Here, Joe raised himself, perched on his elbow, the pain in his back screaming. "Where is God? Where, in all this is He? Under the table? Behind the door? Is He in that little bathroom? It seems He's hiding."

Ellie kept her voice even. "God never hides, though there are times it can seem so. In Isaiah, we're told he will be with us as we go through deep waters. The waters are deep for you right now."

"The waters aren't the only thing that's deep. You're piling it up pretty deep in here pastor."

"Joe, you've never been a cynic, nor one to give up. What has changed?"

"Are you seriously asking me that?"

"The core of you is still there; I know it. You are still the person who has contributed so much for others. If you remain steadfast as I have always known you to be, God will take care of you. He rewards those who trust in him rather than their own understanding. He has rewarded you in the past. You've had a good life, haven't you?"

"I think 'had' is the important word there."

"You'll have it again. It may be different, something you cannot even envision right now. But it's coming. God rewards those who remain committed."

"Was I not committed? Or, maybe I should be committed now, to an institution."

Ellie remained quiet for a moment, then led with all she could muster. "Fall back on your faith Joe. You'll find confidence in it, even peace, eventually. Turn to God. He can return to you everything you had, and more."

"Can He return my son?"

Ellie paused, necessarily, knowing what she could not promise, but wondering what she could. "Joe, like you said, I cannot even imagine your pain. But in Romans, we're told that the pain we feel now cannot compare to the joy that is coming."

"Joy? I see no joy in my life."

"You'll find it again. You and Sophia together. She'll still need you when this is over. You can lean on each other."

"You heard what she said."

"Yes."

"I lost my child and she would throw herself away behind him. She'd leave me with nothing. Less than nothing. Pain. I can't not think about it. I can't think of her without that image. And I can't think of him without pain worse than you can imagine. So, if you don't mind, I'd like some nice drugs so I don't have to think about anything."

"Your pain will be here when the meds wear off. Why not face it now, with your faith intact?"

"My faith is the same as it always was. My body is no longer intact.

Nor my mind. So, I'd like to turn both off."

"The doctors can help you with the mind and body. I am concerned for your soul."

"Just go. Now, please." Joe's voice was thin, and he was wracked with a series of coughs, each of which sent waves of pain through his back. The shudders did not stop the coughing fit, but sent him into near convulsions, his body trembling, his eyes clouded. His vision of Ellie was obscured. As she stood to go, his image of her from below was that of a monstrosity, looming over him menacingly. Her humanity had disappeared; in its place was nothing he recognized, kindness and empathy now being unimaginable. "Go," he managed weakly.

"I'll go," she responded, "but now that you need to take a breath for a moment, I'll use this moment to impart some final thoughts. I hope you have the patience for them. I don't claim to have all of the answers, but I know a bit about the secrets of God's kingdom. During my time as a pastor, I've had a number of occasions to encourage members of the church to repent, to rethink their ways of reasoning. I've never had such a concern with you Joe. You've always been one of those holding up others. But I am forced to wonder about the path you're traveling. Your discouragement verges on foolishness. God doesn't just provide and encourage, in Joshua, He commands us to be strong and courageous, whatever adversity we face. I cannot tell you what might have led to the misfortunate you've endured recently. But I can only tell you this. Look into your own heart. The answer lies there.

Ellie exited the room, closing the door loudly and firmly as she left. Her departure provided Joe with the darkness he craved, though there was no peace in it.

CHAPTER 6

The pastor had called, so Billy knew her attempt at comfort had been a failure, but it didn't diminish his confidence. He'd known Joe since high school and knew his moods. If anyone could get him back on track, it would be Billy. He'd been doing this half his life.

Not that Joe was prone to mood swings or depressive episodes. Quite the contrary. His stability had never been in question, and Billy took that as a point of personal, though quite private, pride. Billy had always been the facilitator in their relationship, the point guard to Joe's scorer on the team, the background horn while Joe took the solos with the band. Lately, Billy's trombone had been silent by choice, except on the rare occasions when he needed to demonstrate something to the kids the foundation supported. The longer he'd been with the organization, the more uncommon those occasions became. Basketball was now limited to the occasional one-on-one with Joe at the gym or one of the local street courts.

So, it was with empty hands and a determined mind that Billy stepped out of his Honda Civic and walked through the parking lot, into the elevator, then down the hall to Joe's room where his friend awaited.

"Billy, I don't know what you're doing here. You should be looking for a job," Joe finally said after several minutes of silence. Billy could endure the silence. Among good friends, it is rarely awkward.

"I have a job," Billy's response was as quiet as the situation demanded.

"In case you hadn't heard, the company is near bankruptcy. The foundation will close. Lawsuits are on the way, if they haven't been filed already. Those loggers."

"Those employees will be remembered for doing important work. Their families will be taken care of."

"I don't recall you working on that side of things. Did you join the legal or accounting team while I've been laid up? Last I heard, you were on the arts initiative, not that I've heard a peep from your horn in years."

"My horn has never 'peeped' in its long and distinguished life. It has howled, growled, and occasionally wailed. If I'm having an off day, it might hiss. But it never peeps."

"When is the last time it left your closet?"

"When are you leaving here? Most of your physical wounds seem to be healing. Is the doc not releasing you?"

"That's between me and the doctor. You can go now. I might need to do some howling, growling, and wailing myself, and I'd rather not have an audience."

"Your best friend is hardly an audience. I'd like to think that other than Sophia and..."

"Don't say his name!"

Billy put his hands up in the universal gesture of remorse, but didn't back off. "You'll have to talk about him at some point. And with her."

"Don't tell me what I have to do. You have no idea how I feel."

"I can only imagine."

"No. You can't."

"I know." Billy took Joe's hand, only to have it pulled from him, the intravenous tube clacking against the bedrail.

"You don't know Jack. You sit there and tell me what I should feel, what I should think, what I should do, who I should speak with and about. You know nothing about it, you hanger-on. Is the window open? Because it seems like the wind is blowing pretty strong through here. Everyone who knows nothing about what I'm dealing with seems to know everything about what I should do about it. How is that?"

"Joe, I..."

"You what?" Joe was screaming now, his anguish taking hold, so he figured he may as well give in to it. The pain in his back seemed to envelop his body as he let it out, "Aaagghh." It was loud enough that a nurse's aide peered into the room, considered adjusting his pillows, but decided against it, moving on to the next room.

"Do you need some meds? I can call someone?" Billy was uncomfortable, perhaps for the first time in their friendship.

"The pain I'm feeling can't be resolved by medication."

"Joe, you're the strongest person I know."

"What do you think I'm made of? Stone? Brass, like that horn of yours? There are limits and I've hit mine."

"You never know what you are capable of until you're tested."

"This is the test? If so, I've failed."

"Don't give up so easily."

"Easily? You think any of this is easy? We copied each other's homework enough in high school. Does this look like any of those assignments? If so, teach me, because I'm all out of answers."

"I don't have answers for you, Joe. You've always been better at the big ideas than I am. Build on the foundation you've set, your values, your innovation. You'll come up with something."

"My foundation? What is that?"

"I don't know, Joe. It's just that part of you that I've always followed. Your instincts, I guess. You've never steered me wrong."

"Well, I'm no longer steering, so you'd better get off this train quick as you can."

"I think you're mixing your metaphors."

"Go home, Billy. Look for a job."

"I have a job. With you."

"We're going in circles. The company is kaput; it will be bankrupt within a month. The job you've had for the past decade is gone. The arts program, the forest. God, the forest. We've made the very problem we were trying to solve much worse."

"You don't know everything yet. Not all the information is in."

"You see the news yesterday?"

"I try to avoid it when I can."

"You no longer have that luxury. Seriously, Billy, you've been a good friend, but we can't pay you to manage an arts program that will no longer exist. Pull that trombone out of your closet. Make a living with it."

"Like I told you, I do have a job. It's just not the one you thought. My job was never just to work for the foundation, to create and maintain an arts program, to teach kids, or any of that. My job was to be your friend, help implement your vision."

"My vision is hazy now. You'll have to find your own dream, your own vision."

"Never had one Joe, nor needed one. For now, I'm going to trust that yours will soon come back into focus. I've seen people doubt you before and later they were ashamed about it." Billy got up from his chair, kissed his friend on the forehead, and took a step toward the door. "Gotta go Joe, but I'll be back. I know you think the world has cast you aside, and maybe the path out of this isn't clear to you yet, but it will be. The world doesn't throw away the good ones, Joe. You have to find where you fell off the path. It will come to you."

Joe just stared in silence as Billy left the room. Stepping into the elevator, Billy caught his breath. For the first time in a long time, he was troubled. Uncertainty did not suit him.

CHAPTER 7

Zaida was armed, though she was sure she needn't be. Joe wasn't

her enemy, never had been. He was closer to a mentor, though that

was a relationship she didn't easily admit. Ego was something she

didn't hide well, nor ambition for that matter.

But her arms were metaphorical, paperwork showing the

devastating impact of the multiple crises the company had suffered

in the last few days. She was little involved in the charitable work Joe

and his friends performed with a portion of their earnings, but she

understood the foundation's work enough to include it in the

paperwork she was carrying. She trailed the little cart of documents

behind her, through the elevator doors, down the hallway to visit her

friend and transact a little business.

There is, unfortunately, little way to be armed to meet with a brick wall, which is what Zaida encountered. Joe's tone was mocking, from the outset.

"It doesn't matter. None of it matters."

"Of course it does. We have a lot we need to go through and I know you're tired, but I've simplified as best I can. If you could just let me..."

"Take your papers and go home. There's nothing I can do about any of this."

"There's always something you can do. I know the choices aren't ideal, but..."

"Not ideal? As I recall, the stock plummeted to...what's below nothing?"

"The company still has value. There are assets."

"Really? Do we have customers, a market? I believe we have a building and a warehouse or two of worthless panels."

"I'm surprised at you. You always said the people are our biggest asset."

"I don't remember. I'm not much for corporate cliches."

"Thought you meant that one."

Perhaps I did. It's meaningless now. You do good, you do bad, it doesn't matter. Either way, what you do gets destroyed."

"Whether you think it matters or not, there are details to be worked out. If you would just let me go over some things."

"I won't. I'm tired. I'd like to be left alone. None of those papers matter to me, the company doesn't matter. I don't matter. Even my clothes seem to hate me."

"Your clothes? Now I'm confused."

"Confusion is my new way of life. I'm learning to live with it. I don't know why I was even born."

"Bitterness doesn't become you sir."

"Bitterness! You want to hear bitterness? All I've worked for, gone. In minutes, just gone. My career. My reputation. The company. The foundation. All gone. Any purpose any of them ever had is gone. I don't know what purpose they ever served." Joe pushed the papers off the table. Zaida caught them deftly amid her confusion. "Go away Zaida and turn off the light as you go."

"Your reputation? I've never taken you for vain."

"Vain?"

"You can't even see it. Your eyes are failing, along with your moral center."

"I'm not fighting with you anymore," he said wearily. I feel no need to justify myself. I couldn't if I tried."

"Sir…"

"If you call me that one more time…"

Zaida stood. She picked up the paperwork, none of it having been read, much less discussed. "I've never seen such insanity," she said coldly. "I wish I had some secret lesson to share with you, but you don't seem to be able or willing to hear it. When you're ready, it will be there for you. Just look around."

"Go," he said.

She went, turning out the room light as she departed, leaving Joe to his darkness.

CHAPTER 8

A week after the accident, Joe and Sophia both left the hospital, but not together. Each had been approved for release by their respective physicians but they had no contact. Only one day previous, Sophia had asked to be taken down to Joe's room. She called from the door, softly at first, then, louder. Joe was oblivious, or appeared so. Through their stays, he refused all contact.

Sophia's new Prius had already arrived, the insurance details to be worked out later. She took the new key fob in her hand as the attendant wheeled her downstairs, her belongings in a plastic bag in her lap. With the fingers that peeked out of the cast on her right hand, she played with her wedding ring on her left. It was no looser nor tighter than it had been before the accident, the scars on her fingers notwithstanding. She stepped carefully and resolutely up to the curb and opened the car door, turned and thanked the orderly with a brief smile, sank down into the seat, adjusted the mirrors, and, looked back only once at the building that had been her residence for the last seven days. It still held the man with whom her life and dreams had been built. She drove out of the parking lot and south toward their home on Good Hope Circle.

A few hours later, Joe took the same ride down the elevator in a similar chair, to a waiting car he'd arranged through Lyft. The matching plastic bag in his lap held his own wedding ring, along with his clothing and what few items he had with him. He stepped quietly into the back seat of the Lyft, confirmed his identity and destination with the driver, and leaned back to shut out the sounds of the city. He accepted the pain that shot through his back with every bump of the road as his fate in life, and perhaps his identity. The car weaved through the South Bay traffic toward the nearest Best Western, where he hoped to find another level of darkness to shut out the world.

CHAPTER 9

Ellie went over the spreadsheets one more time. They said the same thing they had the last five times she'd reviewed them. Allowing the church budget to become too reliant on the donations of any one family had to be the worst mistake she'd made as a pastor. In a separate file, she had compiled a list of community programs that would have to be cut if the Taylor family were indeed bankrupt, as was the rumor.

Joe came rambling around the corner, in a rumpled sweatshirt over a pair of jeans, an equally rumpled look on his face. He sat in one of the two chairs opposite Ellie without uttering a word.

"So…" Ellie began.

Joe remained silent. After several moments, he looked up, a mild questioning look on his face, then down again.

"Joe," she began again. "I know you have many things going on."

Joe humphed sarcastically, but remained silent.

"Your business, the details of which I've never known fully, your charities, yes, a lot." Ellie looked down, but still got no response.

"For now, perhaps we can focus on your marriage. How is Sophia?"

"I wouldn't know."

"And, why wouldn't you?"

"You know, I hate when you do that."

"Do what Joe?"

"Ask questions you know the answer to. It's condescending."

"What makes you think I already know?"

"Because I know you. I'm sure you've already spoken with Sophia."

"I have. The question is, why haven't you?"

"You know why."

"I know you're hurting, Joe. Don't you think she's hurting as well?"

"I'm sure she is."

"I've never known you to be callous or unfeeling. What has changed?"

Joe looked up. "Can you even ask me that?"

"Apologies, let me ask a different question. Do you blame Sophia for the accident?"

"Of course not."

"Then, why the anger? Why aren't you with her, grieving together?"

"You know what she said."

"I do. She told me."

"I can't look at her. I can't think about her. I've lost the most important thing ever and she wanted to double it."

"I don't think that's what she said, Joe."

"The effect is the same."

"I don't remember you being so rigid or harsh, with her, or with anyone else."

"There has to be a first time."

Ellie said nothing; she had learned that silence was the best way to draw a parishioner out. Joe waited as well, nothing seemed on his mind, or everything. Finally, she lost patience with her own silence. "You know I've counseled many couples. How can we bring the two of you back together?"

"There's no bridge that wide or that strong, pastor. She kicked it aside and it can't be rebuilt." Joe paused. Summoning his last reserves of energy, he returned to the metaphor. "I can't rebuild that bridge; the chasm is too wide and too deep. And, if I look back, I'll fall through. Every time I even think about it, I lose my breath."

Ellie held up her hand in a way that was uncharacteristic, but felt necessary. "Yes Joe, I know, the level of pain you're experiencing is beyond anything I could imagine. But, Sophia is still Sophia. And aren't you still the kind, compassionate man who committed your life to hers?"

"Returning to condescension I see."

"Joe, I don't mean..."

"No, you don't. But you seem to think you know people better than they know themselves. You don't. I'm sorry pastor, but God hasn't gifted you with any special insight along with those robes. I think I know more about my marriage than you do, and far more about my business and foundation, in case you were thinking of bringing up those." Ellie winced and resisted the urge to glance down at the newspaper article in her drawer.

"Do you know about God, Joe?" Ellie thought herself on firmer ground, but even she sensed the defensiveness in her retreating voice.

"God?" Incredulous wasn't the word to describe his tone any longer. "I know you think you have some special knowledge there, being a pastor and all, but you don't. I'm not blind. I have as much insight into God and the havoc He wreaks as you."

"Joe, if you turn to God..."

"I'm done turning. I've been turning like a pig on a spit for weeks." He pulled up his shirt, showing Ellie the scars. He got the wince he was expecting. "See, I know what God does."

"Your injuries, and all that has happened, are acts of men, of people, not God. What God does, what God is, is love."

"Does...allows. Is there a difference really?"

"Joe, you certainly cannot hold God responsible for what has happened to you."

"God is all powerful, all wise, so why not? Isn't he responsible for everything?"

"God gave us free will, Joe."

"What the hell for? You've seen how we use it, abuse it. We kill each other, rape the environment, destroy his creation. In what wisdom does he trust us?"

"Humans do all those things Joe, and they disturb God a great deal. They break his heart. But it would be fallacy to hold God responsible for them. They're not His work."

"Aren't they? If he created us, and we do these things. It's the same thing. *He allows it* is the same as *He does it*."

"He also allows or does wondrous things. Have you forgotten those?"

"Yeah, they seem to be slipping my mind at the moment. Maybe they burned in the fire with that forest I was trying to preserve."

"I'm aware of that situation. I do sympathize. I wish there was something I could do."

"Why don't you pray?" The sarcasm dripped from his voice like spoiled molasses.

Ellie occasionally found that earnestness was a convenient refuge. "Will you pray with me Joe?"

"Not today."

"I understand. And God also understands when we're not in the right mental or emotional place for prayer. He hears us nonetheless." She took a breath before changing tack. "Joe, I wanted to come back to the beautiful and wondrous things God creates and allows. You know of course, that your relationship with Sophia, your son, these are among those beautiful things?"

"One of those is no longer here, the other doesn't seem so beautiful anymore."

"Couldn't it again? Couldn't it be restored, even if it isn't the same?"

"Can you roll through a mud puddle, and come out the other side clean?"

"Joe, I don't even know what that means."

Joe stood, shoulders hunched, voice depleted. "It means Pastor, that while I appreciate your efforts, I can't make any of my own. The kind of restoration you suggest is beyond my imagination."

"Joe..."

"I thank you Pastor. Have a good day." With that, he stepped out of her office and out the door.

Ellie stood, looked after him, then sank back into her seat. She touched the computer mouse, activating her screen where the spreadsheet reappeared. She minimized the screen, folded her face into her hands, took a shallow breath, and quietly resumed praying for the wrong things.

CHAPTER 10

Billy stared into the distance, squinting. Yes, that was Joe. It was unlike him to be late. In fact, the two had so often been in sync, going to their days of high school ball, it had become a running joke among their friends. If they agreed to meet at a certain place and time, they'd nearly always arrive at the same moment, neither early, nor late, though they were coming from different parts of town. And on the court, Billy's passes were invariably in the right spots. Joe, of course, was the scorer, and it was Billy's job to set him up, which he did with unconscious accuracy.

As Joe walked closer, Billy felt his chest tighten. He'd never seen his friend look so ragged. He was wearing sweatpants that looked like they'd been lived in, and slept in, for days. And a t-shirt with yellow stains near the top; Billy wasn't sure whether they were food or drool, and he wasn't sure which he preferred.

Joe was squinting, though he wasn't the one facing the sun. Billy heaved a chest pass his way, right at the prime spot as always. Joe put up his hand just enough to knock the ball down. He made no effort to collect it, much less do anything with it. The ball rolled away, coming to a rest behind the basket.

"Don't take this the wrong way Joe, but you look like crap."

"Thanks Billy. Appreciate the support."

"Seriously, how are you feeling?"

"Broken, torn, like those scars on my back. And you?"

Billy ignored the question, knowing there was no curiosity in it. He walked over, picked up the ball, took three dribbles, paused as if to consider a shot, then tossed it to Joe. "Heads up," he called out.

Joe caught the ball this time, sat down near the top of the key, and threw it aside so indolently that it slowed to a roll before reaching his long-term point guard.

Billy picked up the ball, held it under his arm, and walked over, standing in front of his friend, watching, searching for his words. "Dude" he said, not knowing whether it was a question, a statement,

THE BOOK OF JOE

or a label.

"Eloquent as always, Bill." Joe said. But he summoned the energy for a moment of forgiveness. "Don't worry about it. Anything you say today would be in vain, fair warning."

Billy put the ball under his foot, then reached down with both arms and lifted Joe to eye level. His friend didn't help, but neither did he resist this time. "You look like you've been crying."

"Incorrect. I'm cried out. Now, I'm just numb."

"Joe, I've never seen you without that light in your eyes. Where is it?"

"Gone."

"I can't believe that." Billy grabbed the ball, and this time, placed it into Joe's hands. "Take a shot."

"I don't think there are any shots left in me."

"Take a shot Joe."

A flash of anger appeared in Joe's eyes. "You take a shot," he insisted, passing the ball back.

Billy took no shot; he rarely had, even in high school. "Do I need to carry you," he said, hoping to keep things lighthearted. "Like I did back then. I think more than half my assists went to you senior year. Your beast of burden."

"You were the one I could count on back then."

"Still can, Joe."

"I don't know. You don't know what I've lost."

"I know. I mean, I can't imagine, but I do know, if that makes any sense."

"It doesn't."

"You always had the answers, Joe. All the way back."

"Not anymore."

"You still have a lot going for you. Sophia, for example."

The anger was back, though Joe refused to address it directly. "I've lost everything Billy, you know that. My son, my business, the good work we were doing, just about every friend."

"Focus on what you still have. Sophia is waiting. I'm here."

Joe took the ball, a glare in his eyes. He passed it to Billy and demanded, "take the shot."

Billy passed the ball back and Joe tossed it lazily toward the basket, an airball. Billy caught it again, and bounce-passed it seamlessly to

Joe. "Try again."

"Why, Bill. What's the point?" He passed the ball back, only to have it returned to him.

"Does there have to be a point? Sometimes, there is no point. Sometimes, the pointless is the point." He collected the rebound, sent the ball again Joe's way again for another shot.

"I don't know what that means. I've never done pointless in my life and you know that." Joe sighed. His third shot missed its mark, the rebound bouncing his way quickly with a small nudge from Billy.

"Maybe that's the problem."

"What are you doing Billy, going to analyze me?"

"Nah, I've never been the one with the answers Joe, that was you. I pass, you complete. It's our way."

"Why is it our way, Billy? Why does it have to be? Why do you never take a shot? You know you had the highest field goal percentage of all point guards in the league two years in a row."

"That's because I rationed my shots."

"Bullshit. You took them only when you had to. Only when I put the ball in your hands and you were right under the basket. When you had no other logical choice but to shoot or coach would have been on your case."

"You were the scorer, Joe. I was the passer." He passed again, the ball hitting the back of Joe's left hand. As it bounced back his way, Billy looked at it, not knowing what else to do. He sent it back to Joe.

Joe tossed the ball toward the basket again, with so little effort it barely touched the rim. Billy collected it and tossed it back. "You want me to analyze you Joe, here it is. You've always known what to do, always had all the answers, now you don't. And it seems that little fact has you a bit lost."

"That's your analysis? Don't quit your day job Billy."

"I work for you, in case you don't remember."

"Oh yes, I guess that means you need to get a job. The foundation will be closing, in case you hadn't heard. You're going to have to step up and find a life. Take your shot."

"It's not my shot Joe, it's always been your shot." With that, Billy bounced the ball back to his friend, only to have it ignored once more. Joe stepped up to him, toe to toe in a way neither could have previously imagined.

"Why do you never take a shot?"

"You're lost Joe. Confused. How can I help?"

"You can't. Shoot the ball."

"I don't want to, never did."

"Why is that?"

"No idea. I told you, you were the one with all the answers. Now you don't have them and it scares you to death. Shoot the ball Joe. You know how and where."

"I don't." With that, Joe put the ball on the ground. He continued to look at Billy, though not in the eye. Billy could see his stare was a bit off center, and wavering.

"You're trembling Joe. Are you eating? Drinking? Or are you living off caffeine and dark thoughts?"

"Don't try to analyze me Billy. You aren't very good at it."

"No, I'm not. Like I said, you were always the one with all the answers. You knew what college we should go to, and I followed. When problems came up in the business, you knew how to solve them. The foundation, you knew which direction it should take. It was never me. I followed where you led. Always."

"You never had a problem with it before. Why now?"

"Still don't have a problem, Joe. I'm grateful. Always have been. If not for you, I'd still be another broke kid from Tulare playing a little ball, a little horn, and not knowing what to do with my life."

"So, that's the deal? I lead, you follow? I score, you assist? When are you going to make decisions for yourself. When did you last have that horn out?"

"My trombone is in my closet. These days, I help others play, you know that. But right now, I'm worried about you. Life seems to have thrown you one curveball too many."

"You're mixing your metaphors Billy. Neither of us has played a minute of baseball in our lives."

"You know what I mean. Every step of the way, you've known what to do. I've been along for the ride, if you don't mind another metaphor. I'm here asking, waiting for your next move. What's it going to be?"

"No idea. You decide."

"I'm here to support you, Joe. Just tell me how."

Joe looked down for a moment, tried and failed to set his jaw and stop himself from trembling, then looked back up. "I have no worldly idea, Billy. I've made my bed and right now, it looks like a grave. Maybe I'm ready for it. If you're not going to take your own shot, feel free to lie in it with me."

Billy opened his mouth to protest as Joe walked away, the ball falling between their feet. He had no words. He stared after his friend, then walked away, the ball sitting unmoving on the court, just behind the free throw line.

CHAPTER 11

Zaida pulled her laptop and briefcase from the trunk of her silver Audi convertible, closed the lid, adjusted her sunglasses and pushed through the doors, smelling coffee and hearing the whir of espresso machines. She glanced back at the car, her one luxury amid a life of practicality. Her reputation for being no-nonsense was well earned.

Unfortunately, she'd already had to deal with a heavy dose of nonsense just to get this meeting with Joe. He'd first refused to even leave his hotel room and hung up on her when she suggested he come to the corporate offices. The compromise, after rounds of negotiations that rivalled the Paris Accords, was the coffee shop next to his hotel. She could see him through the window, looking disheveled and staring at the table. He had lost weight since she'd last seen him, his shirt was hanging loosely, his skin seeming to cling to his bones.

She managed to keep the sarcasm out of her voice as she put her things down. "How are you, Joe? Can I get you anything?"

"No, let's just get this over with."

Zaida put her latte down and pulled out her folder of paperwork. "OK, right down to business. I've prepared most of the bankruptcy paperwork, actually, a few different versions, depending on some decisions you need to make. I know you, so I figured you'd care most about taking care of the employees, so let's start with this one." She placed her first option in front of Joe; it wasn't her favorite, but she was sure it would be the one he preferred, and thought it best to save time. Based on their phone conversations, she wasn't sure she could keep his attention for long.

Joe didn't look up.

"As you know, there aren't any good options, but this one creates the least pain for employees in all of our locations. It prioritizes their contracts, at least those who have them. The downside is that, well, for those of us at the top, the payout for the next few months isn't as great. But, we do have to keep enough of us here to get things closed out. Joe are you listening to me?"

"Not really." Joe's voice was matter of fact and not in the least apologetic.

"Joe, this is serious. I know you're depressed, and you have...family stuff going on, but this company is your life's work. At least your life so far. I don't know what's next for you, but this is over. The stock price dropped so low the company isn't worth much more than the building we work in. There's no coming back from this, not with the new trade agreement. Our business just can't compete with the new rules. We have to dissolve."

"Not dissolving the company."

"Joe, there's no other way. We can't stay in business. The only way to keep going would be to move our production overseas, not China, but maybe Bangladesh or India, and I know that's not something you're willing to consider."

"You're right about that."

"So, we're agreed then. Dissolving the corporation is the only way. The question is just which plan we want to present to the bankruptcy court. Of course, they don't have to accept, but we should put our best foot forw—"

"No bankruptcy."

Zaida was getting exasperated. "Joe, I'm not sure I understand. Do you have some kind of secret plan of which I am unaware? Because the clock is ticking on this, and we need to…"

"*Your* clock is ticking. I am not involved."

"Joe, you're the CEO. Regardless of what else is going on in your life, you have a responsibility to the organization you created. To the people who've come to depend on you. To the board."

"The board is a bunch of rich assholes who come together out of legal necessity."

"If you like, I can share that sentiment with them."

"Feel free."

"Joe." She almost wanted to reach out and take his hand, but Zaida Choksi was not the touchy-feely type. At this moment, she would rather have taken him by the shoulders and given him the kind of hard shake her mother was known for. She restrained herself, admirably, she thought. "Joe, our choices are limited here. Now, other members of the executive team have reminded me that you are known for working miracles, so I'll give you that chance. Do you have some other plan that I should be aware of?"

"None."

"So Joe, what it is you expect us to do? What do you want *me* to do?"

"Find a way."

"A way to do what?"

Joe finally looked up and seemed to summon a reserve of energy. "To stay in business, keep production here, keep the employees, keep producing those panels, keep the foundation operating, stop global warming while you're at it."

"You know that isn't possible."

"Maybe it's not. I certainly have no idea. But I will not sign the death warrant of this company. I won't do it."

"Joe, you have to." This time, she came close to touching him.

"Have to? Who do you think you're talking to?"

"I know my place, Joe. I've always been the pragmatic one; it's why you brought me on board. To temper your idealism and introduce a little reality once in a while."

"Right now, I'm rethinking that decision. You've made yourself a stranger to me."

"Look, I'm on board with all the work you've been doing. I'm as concerned about the environment as the next person. But in this market, we can't compete." She pulled out her laptop. "Look, I'll show you the numbers. They're paltry and you know it."

Joe snapped Zaida's laptop closed, almost pinching her fingers in the process. "I don't have the time to look at numbers right now."

"The time? With all due respect, it seems that time is all you have right now. What have you been doing with yourself. No, strike that, none of my business. But this company is very much my business. As CFO, it is my responsibility..."

"To what? To break me into pieces?"

"You or the company Joe?"

"They're one and the same and you know it."

"You've always called me the workaholic. You on the other hand, had more balance. Even as CEO, you managed to have other interests. Your family, the foundation."

"Both gone, don't vex me by reminding me."

"I can't and won't speak to your family situation. I'm single by choice, so I have little experience in such things. But we're boxed in here, Joe."

"No, you're boxed in. Don't put fences around me."

"Look, I know what they're saying in the financial press, that the bloom is off the rose, that your star no longer shines, but you've always been immune to such things. It's one of the things I've liked about working with you, one of the few things we have in common."

"So, take the job yourself, the glory and all."

"Joe, I don't want to be CEO. Not that I don't have ambitions, but I know my skills, and they're better suited to what I'm doing now."

"And what is that? Lecturing me without listening? You haven't heard a word I've said, not one."

"Joe, you're leaving me without options."

"There are always options. I just don't know what they are this time. You find them."

"I wouldn't even know where to look. Joe, if you think there's something we can do, I'm all ears. But if not, I need you to sign one or another version of these plans."

"I'm not signing."

"I've worked for you for a while now, even considered you a friend." Zaida paused. "And as you know, I don't have many friends. But you're not leaving me many options here. If you won't listen to reason, I'll have to take this to the board."

Joe waved her on, dismissively. "Go. Do what you need to do."

"What I need to do? You know what this would mean? Not just for the company, but for you, for your image. Not only will the media darling's little crown be ripped from your head, you'll be a laughingstock. College kids will study you as an example of corporate stubbornness, their professors will ridicule you. What about you, Joe?" This was Zaida, speaking as a friend, her version of compassion.

Joe looked up but briefly. "Feed me to the worms for all I care."

Zaida was speechless, if for but a moment. "You know what this means, Joe. I'm sorry, but you've done it to yourself." Zaida packed up the unexamined papers neatly, picked them up along with her laptop. She left the latte untouched, thinking Joe likely needed it more than she did.

After packing everything in her trunk, and heading out on the highway, Zaida began to plan. It wouldn't be pleasant, but she knew exactly what she had to do, and she took her responsibility seriously.

CHAPTER 12

No one saw a little boy wandering the streets of San Jose that early morning. Or Morgan Hill. Nor any of the towns and cities in between, the ones that rub against one another like nondescript urban furrows of different colors, shapes, and sizes. Yet both Joe and Sophia experienced something. As neither professed a belief in ghosts, perhaps it was a shared dream. After all, both were in bed at the time.

Sophia saw the child in the doorway of their shared bedroom on Good Hope Circle. He looked her way, eyes bright and questioning, his teddy bear in hand. Minutes passed as each stared at the other. Sophia called to him, invited him over, and waited patiently as he stood, resolute, neither leaving, nor joining her. Finally, as the image began to fade, she started awake. Looking around the room, she burst into tears, her grief renewed, then pulled Joe's soft, heavy duty pillow toward her, hugged it close as if it were her husband's shoulders and torso, and sobbed into it until sleep arrived again.

In the waning hours of the morning, the same vision came to Joe, those identical bright and questioning eyes, calmly waiting in the doorway of his motel room, looking at Joe, but neither coming to his side, nor making a move to leave. As the child waited, Joe stared, his rage building. His awareness of the apparition's unreality fed his adrenaline, yet words failed him. He turned to the doorway just as the child began its fade, its diminishing aspect further enraging Joe, who grabbed a shoe from the floor and threw it toward the door, which it missed. The curtains to the window fell back, parted, and a crack formed in the window, through which the morning light would stream every remaining day of Joe's stay at the motel, depriving him further of the sleep he needed.

No one saw a child, traveling alone, leaving neither an upscale neighborhood in Morgan Hill, nor a downtown motel in San Jose. It seems most likely he was never there, that his appearance in the disparate doorways was a figment, or perhaps figments, in the imagination of two differently grieving parents. Or, perhaps, given that their once strong connection had been severed, it could be that the figments were not in the imagination of the parents, feeding their minds, but in ours, based on the holes of our own we need those figments to fill.

CHAPTER 13

Ellie opened wide the door of the fellowship hall, smiling broadly. She was determined to connect with Joe, this time on a personal level. In doing so, she'd ignore his newly found cynicism, focusing on the person she had known for several years. Joe was a giver. He found his purpose in helping others. It should have already occurred to her that facilitating the act of helping would be the path to reaching him.

Still, she was shocked to see his condition. He'd lost weight, and his face was gaunt, the skin slack. She had spoken with his friend Billy, who shared her concerns, but had few answers. Zaida, whom she'd also met at the hospital, she'd been unable to reach. Ellie masked her worries as she greeted her congregant.

"Hey Joe. I'm glad you could stop by."

"I'm still not sure why I'm here. What's the emergency?"

"I don't think emergency is the word I used," Ellie lied. I said we needed your help urgently. As you know, Friday is our day to feed the unhoused, and several of our usual volunteers couldn't make it.

"Today is Friday?" Joe asked, without curiosity.

"Indeed it is, and we're a bit behind. It's time to serve. I know it's been a few years, but you remember how this goes, don't you? Just like riding a bike."

"I remember, I guess. But not sure I'm in any shape to help." Joe looked down at his clothes, unconcerned about his appearance, but with the slight hope that it would get him out of this conversation.

"You'll fit right in," Ellie told him, placing an apron over his head and tugging at his elbow. "Come on, we need you serving."

"Couldn't I wash dishes instead?"

"Nope. We need help out here. Plus, I think you could use the human interaction."

Ellie walked up to the serving line and took the place of one of the volunteers, who she sent back to the dishes. She grabbed the tongs to hand out roast beef, then paused a moment to guide Joe to the spot on her left and place a spoon in his hand. "Mashed potatoes, easy as pie," she said. "Though unfortunately, we don't have any pie today. Maybe next time."

Joe took the spoon and plopped down a huge portion of potatoes onto the plate of the man in front of him before Ellie even got the meat on his plate. "Whoa there, you know how this goes. We need to have enough for everyone; plus, gotta leave some room on his plate for the salad and roast."

"Guess I should pay attention. This will be me in a month or two."

"I doubt that Joe, but as we often say, *there but for the grace of God . . .*" Joe grimaced and looked the other way.

"You know Joe, you and Sophia used to serve here almost every week. You've gotten away from it. Any idea why?"

"Maybe I thought I could do better by donating. Since the company went public, I've had more money than I've known what to do with, and less time."

"You've certainly been successful. And, you've been generous with your wealth Joe. We all know that, and we appreciate it.

Everyone here does."

"I suspect most of those eating today have no idea where their meal is coming from. Or their next one."

"True, but they know what they need to know. That someone in this town cares about them, reaches out, provides."

"In case you hadn't heard, I won't be providing much of anything in the future. May as well tell them." At that, the older man on whose plate Joe had just left a smaller than usual portion of potatoes, looked up with concern.

"How have you been Theo?" Ellie gave the man her brightest smile. He seemed to relax and almost smiled back before moving down the line for his salad and roll. "Be careful what you say Joe. There are many ears here, and some are sensitive."

"What do you not want them to hear? The truth?"

"Joe, I think it's been too long since you've volunteered. You've been generous with your money, but not your time. You used to know these folks, many by name."

"I know them. Like I said, I'll soon be them. They're in every city, under every bridge, groaning in the streets, getting robbed, occasionally getting murdered."

"I see God in them. I believe you used to do the same."

"I haven't seen or heard from God in some time. Not sure I ever did."

"Joe, why don't you come back to church this Sunday? We've been missing you there too."

"So that's why I'm here? So you can get me in a pew, contributing my last dollar to the collection plate before I join this crowd?" The potatoes missed the plate of the timid young woman in front of him. Joe waved her on, unapologetically.

Ellie put her hand on the spoon gently and pried it from Joe's hand as he looked off into the far corner of the room. She dished potatoes onto the woman's plate. "How are you, Josephine? Is your father well?" she said in her calmest voice. Josephine nodded and moved along quickly.

"Joe, I've never before seen you so argumentative. Have you really lost sight of God entirely?"

"Completely. He's gone incommunicado."

"Joe, come to church. He'll commune with you there."

"I'll be sleeping in on Sunday. And every day." Joe gave a mirthless chuckle as another spoonful of potatoes nearly missed a plate, this time being caught by a very attentive and very hungry young man. "I need my rest."

"God will give you rest. In church. And strength."

"He will strengthen me? For what? To what end?"

"So you can get back to doing His work."

"And what is that? Serving the homeless? Becoming the homeless? Same difference."

An older couple was in line, the woman putting her husband's plate forward. Ellie placed some roast beef on the plate, then reached over and grabbed the spoon from Joe's hand once again. She repeated both actions as the woman put forward her own plate, appearing almost apologetic.

"Joe, I'll ask you again to watch your words. I see God in these people, just as I see Him in you."

"You see God everywhere, don't you?" His tone was mocking, but she was determined not to bite.

"I do."

"Is God in these mashed potatoes?" he asked, picking up a heaping spoonful, and letting them drop with a plop, splattering on the already stained shirt of the man in front of him.

"God is everywhere Joe. Yes, he's in the potatoes, when they're served with an open heart. He's in the roast beef, the salad, everything."

"He's in the rolls too, I guess." Joe said, leaving his station and walking down the line. "Bread of life! Manna from heaven!" Joe picked up the bag of rolls and walked down the table, placing one on each plate. Most of those being served already had rolls, so they looked up, startled, confused, some worried they might get into trouble.

Ellie nudged open the door to the kitchen. "Hector, could you trade me places again." Then, walking over to Joe, she tried to grab the bag. "Joe, we don't have enough."

Joe slipped away, moving faster. "You're right, we don't. There will never be enough."

Several of the homeless were holding out their rolls for Ellie to take. She waved them off. "Eat, eat," she insisted.

"Joe, maybe you were right. Maybe washing dishes is a better job for you today."

"We don't have enough, Eleanor. You want to know why?"

"Why Joe?" she replied, taking the bag from him, she found it empty.

"Because this," Joe said, crumbling the last roll to bits and letting the pieces fall to the floor. "Is just a piece of bread."

With that, Joe turned away, pushed through the swinging door. Ellie followed, hoping to get him started on the dishes. Maybe some hot water and hard work would calm him down.

But as she entered the kitchen, the far door was closing shut. Joe was halfway down the street.

Ellie gave a small sigh. She looked over at the dishes, piled higher than they'd been just a few minutes earlier. She knew she had a long day ahead of her. For now, she picked up the broom and dustpan. Before anything else, she had bread crumbs to clean up.

CHAPTER 14

Billy began the call with a joke as soon as Joe picked up. "You'd have been welcome in my apartment. You have been here before."

Joe's response was slow and sluggish as though he'd run a marathon and was spending the afternoon recovering. "I don't want to go anywhere."

"That has to change at some point, doesn't it? You'll need to go see Sophia, tend to the business."

"I have no plans to do either."

"I don't necessarily mean today, but it's been weeks Joe. Sometime soon, you'll need to get back to things, reassess, figure out next steps."

"You do that. When you have it figured out, let me know. I might even take a few of those steps."

"Joe…"

"Billy, you know the next step is yours to take. The foundation is going away; you're going to need to find suitable employment, stand on your own two feet."

"I'm OK for now. I have savings. You know, I've always been conservative with money."

"You don't believe it's over, do you?"

"You've done amazing things before. I'm still hopeful. Besides, I have no idea what to do next if I'm not helping run the foundation."

"I have no rabbits left in me. Time to find your own. Pull out your horn. Half a dozen orchestras would hire you in a minute."

"I'll grab my horn if you visit the office, and Sophia."

"I'm not here to bargain."

"You're not *here* at all, Joe. Though not because you weren't invited. How about it? Pop on over. Or, I'll pick you up."

"No thanks. And, neither my corporation nor my marriage are your business."

"Your corporation provides eighty-five percent of the funding for the foundation that employs me. And as I recall, I introduced you to Sophia and was the best man at your wedding. Seems to me that both are my business."

"Stick to the work you know. Your horn."

"That horn has been in the coat closet for the past seven years and you know it."

"You used to use it in schools. Poor schools with poor kids. Go back to doing that."

"Foundation pays more. I have to keep up this lavish lifestyle." Billy gestured to his modest Mountain View apartment, furnished sparely, but with photos of J.J. Johnson, Wycliffe Gordon, and his other heroes, as though Joe could see through the phone. As he'd been to the place several times, Billy imagined that perhaps he could.

"The foundation ain't paying jack much longer. And, as I recall, we hired you to work with kids. Go back to doing that. You're no longer poor thanks to the foundation. Go help them out. Show them the benefit of your wisdom."

"It's a little late for me to do that now. My skills are rusty. Neither the sun nor moon has shone on my trombone since I packed it in the back of the closet and took the desk job. But you *can* talk to Sophia."

"You talk to her. Or talk to any other woman for all I care. When's the last time you had a date?"

"I don't date much Joe, you know that. I like my life neat and tidy, and women are anything but."

"So don't tell me what to do. Seems you're not hearing a word I say, so I'm not thinking I should take your advice."

"Joe, I've heard every word. I just hate seeing you like this, crawling like a worm, stinking like you haven't bathed in weeks."

"You can smell me through the phone now?"

"I almost can. And I do hear you Joe."

"You don't. No one does. I could scream at the top of my voice if I had the energy and no one in this motel, on this street, or in this town, would hear a thing. I could walk through the town square naked as hell and no one would turn their head."

"I doubt that's true. You always commanded attention."

"Not any longer. Or any attention I might command isn't the kind I'd want."

"Why don't you go for that walk. Clear your head. There's something clean and pure about walking under the stars."

"In case you missed it, we live in an urban area. Not many stars to see, even in the middle of the night."

"So, go back home. Remember those trips we used to take out to the desert? The ones to Yosemite when we were kids? We could do that again, Joe."

"Not today. Not anytime soon."

"Joe, I worry about you. You were the one who always had things figured out. If you don't know what to do, how can any of us?"

"I wouldn't know Billy. When you figure it out, clue me in."

There was a long silence. Each could hear the other's breathing, one labored, the other unsure. "Joe…"

Joe gripped his phone so tightly, Billy could hear the plastic case nearly cracking under the strain. "I gotta go Billy. I'll see you around."

"When Joe? Let's get together."

"We will. Just not sure when. Not sure of anything much these days." With that, the call ended, and Billy stared at his phone a full minute before putting it down on the table, dumbfounded.

Hesitatingly, he walked over to the closet, knelt down, and ran his

hand over the case to his trombone, covered in dust and scratches.

Pulling back, he stood and brushed off his hands, closing the door.

Billy walked over to the window, and stared out, waiting for he knew

not what.

INTERLUDE

Joe had slept perhaps five hours in the last three nights. Before

dawn, he gave up and went out. Lean and scrawny, he startled the

passersby as he left the motel. He walked down the street, miles

across town to the north, wandered several blocks west, then headed

back south, neither knowing nor caring whether he was retracing his

steps. Nothing and everything seemed new.

The streets were nearly deserted at first, the homeless saw him,

recognizing him as one of their own, but keeping their distance. His

grey sweatpants were only a few weeks old, but had yet to be

washed, the smell wafting, and turning away even the most jaded of

noses. This wasn't the best neighborhood, but Joe was beyond noticing and soon it changed, now an older set of residences lined the road, eucalyptus trees leaning over his path as he stumbled over roots where sidewalks had been only blocks before.

Then, as the heat of the day began, he entered the technology district, luxurious, but gated away. At one time, he could have easily crossed those security posts, his recognizable face password enough. No longer.

Professional buildings gave way to restaurants, first upscale ones, fitting the area, mixed in with grab-to-go sandwich shops for those who spent their days in cubicles. Corporate logos flashed by as he walked, his legs rubber from the hours on the road, retail shops of the same national chains mixed with fast food joints even more recognizable for the ubiquity and similarity. The smells permeated his brain only slightly, his appetite gone, not that it would have mattered as he'd brought no money with him, no identification, nothing but the key card from the motel under his left sock, scraping the sole of his foot occasionally.

The afternoon set in, and Joe was facing west, his eyes squinting against the sun, his feet shuffling along the sidewalk of downtown.

The stained sweatshirt he was wearing would have had him sweating had he been drinking much water. As it was, he was at risk of heat exhaustion, yet he trod onward, through the industrial district, past another residential one, and on toward a series of high rises, apartment buildings of fifteen or more stories alongside office buildings of a similar size, with service businesses in the lower stories and in between. The sun began to set as he moved into side streets, unconsciously seeking the shade, zigzagging north a few blocks, then further west, and south over similar blocks.

As the sun slipped behind the lowest buildings to the west, Joe came upon a set of iron railings alongside a staircase leading to a nondescript structure. The name on the door was Oasis and a young woman greeted him as he walked up. A name badge identified her as Evangeline. "Good evening. Are you here for the show?"

Joe blanched. "I have no money, I'm afraid."

"There is no charge at the Oasis. We have funding from generous donors that allows us to exist as a service to the community." When Joe hesitated, perhaps recognizing the stench that was coming from his clothing and person, Evangeline took him by the elbow with a welcoming smile, showing no concern that his funk might rub off on her. "Come," she said, handing him a cup of water. "I haven't heard the pieces to be performed tonight yet, but I'm told they'll be beautiful."

Joe wondered briefly if his own foundation was the source of the funding that allowed this place to exist. He'd been through the paperwork identifying all of the organizations that had been recipients of his largesse but couldn't recall whether one called the Oasis graced those pages. He could have asked Billy, but he hadn't spoken with his friend for several days.

He drank the water slowly, with trembling hands, and walked through the entryway. There was a poster on the wall with a description of the evening's entertainment. The frame was silver, which contrasted with the gold-leaf lettering on the advertisement. The words seemed to throb like veins to Joe's straining eyes. His exhaustion was overwhelming.

"Natural History" was the name of the first piece to be performed, by a composer whose name he couldn't make out; there seemed to be a J in the first name, but the rest was blurry. Joe blinked his eyes several times in an effort to clear the cobwebs. It helped only a little.

The second piece was a partial performance of Tchaikovsky's 4th

Symphony

A young man walked up with a tray and an effortless smile. His

name badge identified him as Kemuel. The tray was split down the

middle, with small cups of red wine on the left, and bread, covered in

some kind of soft cheese on the right. Joe picked one of each and

nodded almost imperceptibly. Kemuel thanked him and moved on to

the next patron, seeming to glide across the floor.

The light dimmed briefly and an announcement came over the

intercom, requesting that guests take their seats as the performance

was about to begin. Joe looked toward the doors, which were just

opening, sapphire-shaped doorknobs on either side. As the doors

opened, the word Wisdom moved to the side of each and Serenity

appeared on the inside panels. Joe walked through the entryway,

realizing all at once that his appearance wasn't up to his usual

standards, or the standards of human decency. He smelled himself

briefly and hesitated, wondering where his seat was, then

remembering that he'd paid for no ticket. It must be open seating. He found a place in the balcony, as far from others as possible. Barely managing to pull down the folding seat, Joe collapsed, his muscles giving in to the fatigue they'd been resisting throughout the day. He wondered if he'd be able to rise from the seat when the show ended.

For the first time in weeks, his mind turned toward Sophia. For years now, she'd been at his side, his source of tranquility as he walked through the world. He wondered where she was, what she was doing. Often, he'd felt such a connection with her that he thought he knew where she was anytime her face came to mind. Tonight, he drew a blank.

The music began without introduction or fanfare. Strings seared their way into Joe's brain, pulling him away from whatever remained of conscious thought. He listed into a nearly catatonic state, brought back into consciousness only with the light tinkling of cymbals, each a tiny impingement on his mind, trying to call his attention to something, the subject of which he could not make out.

Drums pounded for several seconds before the vocalist joined. Her performance was incomprehensible, not because of a language barrier, but because Joe had lost connection to his surroundings.

There were words being sung, but their meaning was lost to him; they went over his head, seeming to embed themselves in the walls and the rapt faces of the other patrons, whose understanding must be greater than his own.

A plucking began, lasting for nearly half a minute before giving way to drums, then strings again. Tears streamed down Joe's face as he lost what remained of his vaunted control. Had he eaten or drank anything other than the water, wine, and bread given him in the foyer, all control of his bladder and bowels would have been lost as well, and he'd have made a mess on the floor, one more worrisome than the stains on his soiled clothing.

Joe lost track of time and place and his own personhood. The tears continued, trailing down the dirt that had collected on his face and neck from the day's walking and the weeks without bathing. He would have been embarrassed had he been conscious of the room or the people only three rows below him.

The orchestra switched to the Tchaikovsky piece without acknowledgement. Joe didn't notice, but as his eyes opened briefly during the finale, he realized the conductor's back was to him, her arms waving, gesticulating in a manner meaningless to Joe, but attached to the movements of the musicians as though invisible string connected them. Both she and they were frenetic now, after a brief slowing down, perhaps catching their breaths. Horns and strings wove together, detailing a path Joe could not follow as it seemed to disappear only moments after it came into his vision. There was beauty in the visual snow before his eyes, colors majestic, though fleeting.

As the cymbals began crashing again, Joe flinched, his reverie disturbed. Drums invaded, louder, giving way to the cymbals, clanging again and again, each time giving Joe a jolt, the tears once again pouring down his face, from a source that could not have been imagined given the extreme dehydration to which he had driven himself. Each clang felt like daggers pounding into his brain, thunder and lightning were making a declaration bold and daring, yet their messages were incomprehensible as though blocked by a source over which he no longer had control or understanding.

Joe lost consciousness, the exquisite pain of the experience overwhelming him. He awoke only with the gentle shaking of his shoulder. It was Kemuel, the same sweet smile on his face. "Did you enjoy the performance?" the usher asked, his face filled with genuine curiosity.

Joe managed a brief nod, then stood, his legs shaky. He noticed the sweat staining the cloth seats of the auditorium, considered apologizing, then walked down the aisle. He must have fallen asleep; everyone else had left. His embarrassment rising, he made his way toward the door, through the foyer, past a smiling Evangeline, and out into the bright lights of the city. He had walked many miles that day, and the path back to his hotel or anywhere familiar was unknown to him. Regardless, he stepped forward, winding his way back just as he had come.

CHAPTER 15

Joe had rarely paid attention to the gossipy version of the news. The financial press had loved him, but his interviews were rare, and they fawned about his success from afar. He engaged with the media only when he thought it could help his business or his charitable endeavors, never for his own purposes.

Now, his name was everywhere, and after a month of avoiding it, the news was in his face daily. When he finally turned on his motel room television, he found that the very pundits who had been promoting him for years were now calling him everything from naïve to selfish, blaming him for the demise of both his corporation and his foundation. He opened his laptop and browsed the internet, finding

THE BOOK OF JOE

more of the same.

He pulled on his sweatshirt and found the last twenty dollar bill in his wallet, then walked three blocks to the mall and purchased every newspaper he could find, whether the audience was local or national.

His impulse had always been to drive the narrative rather than respond to it, do the right thing and let people think what they wanted. It had served him well. But for the first time, he found himself without a voice and resenting it. His name had been dragged through the mud and back again. It was time to pull out a firehose and spray back.

He pulled his laptop open once again, took a big gulp of coffee, and with an intensity he hadn't shown in weeks, began to write.

Editorial: Wall Street Journal, July 6th

Joe Taylor

It seems that just a few months ago, the financial media, including this magazine, couldn't get enough of me. You thought I was brilliant, the great young entrepreneur who'd found the sweet spot between creating a corporate empire and contributing positively to the world.

All of the kings and princes of modern capitalism thought I was the

next big thing. You considered my every word brilliant and each step

I took as smooth as butter. Many of these so-called princes who sang

my praises never had an original thought in their pampered little

heads, but I digress.

My, how the world has changed.

Now, I find myself under rhetorical attack from all sides, though

most of the blowhards criticizing me have never accomplished a thing

in their lives, unless being a blowhard is, in fact, an accomplishment.

In today's world, it's rather hard to tell.

It's true, and it is no secret. Our business is doomed. We cannot

compete with cheap, exploited labor from China under the likely new

trade rules, and, as I've always stated, I'll never have our products

produced there or in any country in which we cannot provide basic

standards of safety for our employees and a neutral, if not positive,

impact on the environment.

This, of course, is the crux of the criticism I'm now receiving. I am

naïve, idealistic, unfit to lead in a modern world, adapt to its complexities. I own it all. I have never been one to accept that a better world is impossible, that we cannot do right and do well, that we must compromise our core values in order to lead and accomplish. Do I want it all? You betcha.

We've compromised enough. The modern global economy, in all of its brilliance, was built on fossil fuels. The entire industrial era came about through their use. We could keep using them forever, except for the annoying little fact that they won't last forever, and that their use is causing rising temperatures in our oceans and atmosphere. Pesky, those details.

I thought we could do more, be better.

I know the arguments currently being made, asinine as they are. On one side, I'm told that my regard for fair compensation and labor standards is outdated, that workers will benefit from living in abject poverty rather than desperate poverty, that safety protocols are an unnecessary waste, given the environmental benefit our products provide. I've even been called nationalistic, or worse, unfairly giving preferential treatment to relatively privileged American workers over those in impoverished nations who need the jobs more. Even if I were to accept this specious argument, the issue has always been one of control. Here, we run our own factories, each facility overseen by our own corporate manager, subject not only to the more rigorous US labor standards, but the higher ones to which we hold ourselves. Shipping those jobs overseas doesn't just mean Americans would lose them. It means contracting out, losing the ability to ensure that those who make our solar panels and related products are treated well, paid adequately, and kept safe.

The other argument is that we should compromise on environmental standards, use materials that are less expensive, saving on cost while degrading the world's rivers and streams. Those making these arguments don't live near the waterways that would likely be affected, but, though I don't either, I refuse to make that concession. There has to be a better way.

The concept that we must compromise our labor standards or our environmental standards is a false choice that has gotten the world into the mess it is in currently. We need bolder, better thinking from our corporate and political leaders. If that leadership comes from someone other than myself, so be it. Surely there is someone out there with the necessary vision to take the next step.

I'm told that my own naïve mistakes led to the current situation, that the new Chinese panels about to overwhelm the market are the result of my unwillingness to make tough decisions, to choose between evils. I reject this position wholesale. If there are only evil choices to be made, I refuse to be a party to making them.

I would be remiss if I did not address what is perhaps the biggest criticism I am facing, that I have abandoned the company, refused to sign the obviously necessary bankruptcy paperwork, that I am holding out for a miracle, or have just gone AWOL. To be perfectly honest, I don't know which of these is more insulting, nor which is more accurate. For me to sign the death knell of the corporate and environmental enterprise I began with such high hopes would be to admit that we cannot achieve a better world, that we are destined to suffer and die in this one. As many of you know, I lost my only son in a recent tragedy, but I refuse to stand by and watch your children live in a world defined by crisis, pollution, environmental degradation, lowered standards, and increasing temperatures. Perhaps it is predestined, maybe it will happen regardless of what I do, but I will *not be the one to affix my name to the death certificate.*

I refuse.

Editorial: Chronicle of Philanthropy, July 8th

Joe Taylor

There has been a great deal of consternation, in these pages, and those of similar publications, about the presumed demise of the Joe and Sophia Taylor Foundation. I have thus far, not commented, and would prefer to continue that silence, as it is my preference to let my actions do the talking when it comes to charitable giving, rather than make announcements.

I will make an exception in this case as there appear to be those of you, who while perhaps well-meaning, are focused on what we may no longer be able to do rather than what you can and must do. So, I will here provide a quick review of some of the activities of our foundation.

We have, for several years, provided services to those with disabilities, including the blind, deaf, and veterans returning with paraplegia, post-traumatic stress, and other conditions. We have done research into and provided funding for, innovative medical devices that assist in minimizing the effects of these conditions and helping people live productive and happy lives.

Will you now provide these services?

We have given resources to after-school programs for poor families, so that the children of single parents can work, attend college, or do whatever is necessary to care for themselves and their children. We have recruited mentors to children without fathers; I once served as one myself. We provided educational resources to those single parents so they could be empowered to improve their circumstances. Further, we did research into the causes of poverty and when politicians tried to enact policies that made it worse, we called them out publicly and shut their mouths. We sat with the poor, prayed with them, grieved with them when it seemed no one was on their side.

Will you make these programs your own?

In the arts, we funded music and theatre programs across the country, not only providing jobs, but giving people the voice they often lack, to create a beautiful, mournful, or visceral record of our *time, in words, songs, and on stage. We donated instruments and also training, at a time when short-sighted politicians cut funding for the arts, as though the most human aspect of being human is an extravagance.*

What of these people who are in need of expression? Will you sing with them, dance with them, jump for joy with them?

When it comes to our natural world, we have done all we can to prevent the destruction of wild, sacred spaces, giving funding for parks in urban areas, as well as the purchase of swaths of forest, keeping them untouched as nature intended. As you might have seen in the news, that effort may have been for naught, but it was well-intended, and the need remains critical. Perhaps it is more so with the loss of areas of land we had hoped to protect in perpetuity. The owls, the lizards, every creature of the forest, has known us as a friend, indeed as a beloved sibling.

With the recent devastation of these forests, will you protect others? Will you plant new trees to replace those lost?

Perhaps you thought I would write here of our plan for the next version of the Joe and Sophia Taylor Foundation. I must tell you, I don't have one. That part is up to you. You can donate to us if you like, to pay off our debts. But I honestly don't know where to go next. You can donate to other places as well.

For the last several years, I have done what I could to give back to the world that has given me so much, in wealth, and in human kindness. I have wrapped myself in the knowledge that we are doing good while doing well, like that knowledge is a warm coat, keeping out the cold complicated reality of our times. While I always tried to remain humble, if perhaps I have taken pride in our accomplishments, it could be that our current powerlessness is my punishment. If so, such understanding is beyond my capabilities and anyone with greater wisdom isn't sending it my way.

Here is all I do know: Our foundation is no longer in a position to do the things upon which so many have come to rely. I am skeptical that we will ever be able to do so again. So, the question to ask yourself is not what we will do to restore these capacities. It is how you can do these things yourselves. Because we no longer can.

The ball is in your collective court. It is your turn.

Editorial: San Jose Mercury News, July 11th

Joe Taylor

I have tended to stay away from the local gossip section, the vicissitudes of which are beyond my understanding, and interest. In the pages of this paper, and other local ones, I was, until recently, the annointed prince, held in high esteem by the young and old, the political right and left, to all those with eyes and ears, it seemed. I always took these ramblings with a huge grain of salt, knowing that they were designed to fill space, and attract readers, not serious journalism.

I think no more highly of recent speculations, though they have turned cruelly in the other direction. Whereas before, I was successful, had the ear of the high and the low, and rode that success to make a difference, in business and in the world, now, I find myself blown about by the wind, with no voice of my own, let alone control of my future.

I doubt many of you want to hear from me. Most likely, any cries I send out will be disregarded, as perhaps they should be, given my life of relative privilege until recently. Still, the physical pain I have been subjected to from recent injuries, ones that make the wearing of

clothing a difficult undertaking, pale compared to my current life,

watching my former wealth pass by like a cloud on the wind, out of

my reach. It seems I'm riding on that wind myself, and perhaps

becoming it, my body and soul fading from existence as few of you

see the real me. Or perhaps I no longer see him.

There has been speculation that I am dying, and at times it has

seemed as though I might die in my little nest here. No, I'm not going

to give you hints as to my current whereabouts, just know that though

your criticism may well bring about my premature death, my days

have recently felt numberless, like grains of sand on the beach.

Perhaps the most painful, and the most ridiculous, of the recent

speculation, has been the comments on my marriage. The assumption

seems to be that because Sophia and I are not in the same building,

there must be infidelity at play, almost certainly on my part. Given the

physical and psychic pain to which I have been subjected recently, the

idea that I would want or need the presence of women, whether from

physical desire or pride, is laughable. If I have ever displayed such

vanity, by all means, show the evidence and judge away. Or, just shut up about it.

It is unlike me to pour out my soul this way, but it seems that too many of you would prefer to tromp it under your feet, until I am little more than dust and ashes so that you can feel better about yourselves for a moment. From the editorials, to the gossip columns, to the letters to the editor, not a single one of you has come to me for my side of the story. I have had no forum, public or private, on which I can defend myself.

So, this is my last defense: Find something better to do.

His vain rantings transmitted, in full knowledge that they would fall on ears deaf by intention, Joe closed his laptop, collapsed on the motel room bed, and closed his eyes as well, sleeping not one minute.

CHAPTER 16

Angel Oritz looked up from her computer screen as she saw Zaida come in. She was friendly and cordial, as always. "Right in here, ma'am. I think you know the way."

Zaida smiled briefly and professionally. "Indeed, I do." Though this was the most consequential board meeting she'd ever attended, she was as prepared as it was possible to be.

Angel opened the door to the boardroom and walked Zaida in. The chief financial officer took a step past the place Angel had laid out for her and set her laptop down in front of Joe's seat at the head of the table. She moved her water glass over to her new spot and sat down. Board members were already quietly filing in.

Before Angel was even out of the room, Zaida had begun the meeting, her tone matter of fact. "None of us wanted to be here today, under these circumstances. But we must take the next steps to preserve the interests of our shareholders and uphold the mission of the company. Joe Taylor is not here and has become unreachable. Sadly, I must now call for a vote regarding a change in leadership."

Angel went back to her desk in the reception area and opened her next file. She had work to do. First, she closed her eyes and took three calming breaths, then opened them again and delved into her labors.

In fewer than fifteen minutes, Zaida exited the boardroom, her face displaying the same unreadable determination. "Have a good day Ms. Choksi," Angel called out, to Zaida's back. Her polite greeting went unreturned. Zaida got into the elevator, pushed the button for the ground floor, and turned around, her face inscrutable.

Angel stepped into the conference room as the board members were packing up their things. She picked up Zaida's water cup and the remains of coffee and pastry dishes used by the board. As she finished packing things away, the snippets of conversation were as she had expected. "jumping the gun...all a bit premature...give him a little more time....he's pulled rabbits out of his hat before....not giving up on him just yet...."

Her service to the board complete, Angel stepped out of the room and walked over to the window. In the parking lot below, she could see Zaida getting into her Audi. She reached into a case above the rearview mirror and pulled out her sunglasses, put them on and adjusted the frames in the mirror. She pulled out of the parking lot, turned left, and entered the freeway heading east. From this point, her shadow never crossed the threshold of Solar Champions again.

Angel paused a moment, took another three breaths, and looked up at the summer sky, closing her eyes for a moment before a final exhalation. She then walked back to her desk and once more set about her work, unchanged from the previous day, or the next.

CHAPTER 17

Restlessness fought with exhaustion and won. Joe once again prowled the streets, his face narrow and haunted behind a cheap pair of convenience store sunglasses. He walked everywhere except where he'd walked before, wanting to confront nothing recognizable.

Nonetheless, familiar sights abounded as the repetitious nature of American corporatism ensured that the same fast-food joints and chain retail stores appeared and reappeared on connecting streets, some just a couple of blocks from their counterparts with little to differentiate them.

Joe fidgeted incessantly, his body fat gone, he was burning muscle rapidly, nervous energy beginning to consume him. He searched for something on which to expend that vigor, finding little other than more restaurants where he could spend money he didn't have. His straining eyes finally rested on a sign saying "In Site Gym;" this was the same chain as the one near his house where he had a membership, though the layout looked different, fewer frills, though there was still the juice bar for those who wanted to tank up after their workout. Surprising himself, he remembered his membership number, gave it to the clerk at the desk and went over to the dumbbells.

Grasping a pair of forty-pounders, he began a set of curls, his torso swinging wildly as this was well beyond his usual weight. Hoping to exhaust himself, perhaps even collapse into unconsciousness, he continued, to twenty reps, then twenty-seven, until his arms couldn't pull the bars up another inch.

Free weights weren't doing it; he moved to the leg press machine, inserting the pin to two hundred eighty pounds. He sat in the machine, and noted a young man in shorts and in "In Site" t-shirt eyeing him as he worked with another client. Joe extended his legs hard and fast, and despite the excess weight, the clang of the bars hitting the top of the machine resounded around the room. Joe hardly noticed, though if he had, it wouldn't have mattered because the bars made the same clang on the way down, which was even faster because he'd never pressed this much before. He pushed again, and the ringing was just as loud. Again, again, both ways, gym patrons started to look his way.

His energy far from sated, Joe moved to the lateral pull-down machine a woman had just vacated, taking her place before she could wipe down the seat. This time, he ignored the weight pins and only three bars went up. They went up fast and the ringing pitched through the room like a frantic church bell. The trainer left his client and came over.

"Look sir," he began, the name Andre emblazoned across his shirt. Joe ignored him, grabbed some dumbbells again and began rapid triceps curls. "Sir, are you all right?"

"I'm not making loud noises anymore, am I?"

"You're not," Andre began, unsure of his next move as rules were no longer being broken.

"Then bug off." Joe's arms were still flailing.

"I'm going, but please be careful, with the weights and the machines. It's about your safety and that of others, not just the noise." Andre turned, but at just that moment, Joe dropped the dumbbell, the heavy weight hitting the floor just between their feet. Joe's fingers were trembling, the ring finger of each hand twitching uncontrollably. "Sir, are you sure you're all right? Have you taken anything? I'm medically trained, so I'm not concerned about busting you, just want to see if we can help."

Joe turned slowly, his eyes locking on Andre's just for a moment before turning downward. "No, I don't think you can help me," he got out, his voice weak and weary. His right arm lifted, appearing at first to have an inclination toward reaching out, then fell to his side. With that, Joe collapsed to the floor, his legs spasming.

Gym patrons began to gather, but Andre waved them away. "Give him space. He's not dangerous. I think he's just dehydrated." As Joe's eyes fluttered, Andre helped him to a sitting position, then after a few minutes, to his feet. Most of the crowd had gone back to their workouts, glancing over between sets. "What you need," Andre began, "isn't more exercise, at least not today. Let's get something in you, preferably liquid."

A half hour later, they were seated across from one another in the corner of the juice bar. Andre was nibbling on an oatmeal bar; he'd have gotten one for Joe, but thought it too much for now. Instead, he'd used his own account to buy Joe a strawberry-banana smoothie, from which he alternated sips with a tall glass of water. Joe looked up, but didn't meet Andre's eyes. Finally, Andre decided it was time. "So, spill it."

"Spill what? Haven't you ever seen anyone a little tired before? By the way, how much was this stuff. I should pay you back once I find my wallet."

"I'm smarter than I look." Andre grasped Joe's chin firmly, but gently and lifted his face up until Joe was forced to stare into his kind brown eyes. He could be patient, but he was persistent. "Tell me. Take your time."

It all came out. The losses he'd not yet been able to say out loud. The advice he'd received with which he could not connect and did not wish to engage. The pain, physical, spiritual, financial, emotional.

The meaningless wandering around the city with a destination neither planned nor arrived at. Joe's voice was raspy and weak, but surprisingly, his resolution seemed to increase as he droned on. Andre looked over Joe's head at the clock; his new friend had been speaking for forty minutes.

"Wow," was all he could say at first. Then, he gathered himself. "So, you've had a lot to say, and I understand, because you've been dealing with a lot. You ready to hear me?"

Joe nodded almost imperceptibly.

"No." Andre pulled Joe's face up to meet his eyes again. "I mean really hear me. Because I think just this once, I have a lot to say.

Joe didn't answer audibly, but Andre went on. "I will start by saying, I know I'm younger than you, younger than most of your friends who've been giving you this horrible advice. They say age brings wisdom, but it doesn't really seem so in this case. Frankly, I think you're all full of crap."

If Joe was startled, he didn't show it. Andre beckoned over to the barista behind the counter and motioned for a smoothie for himself and more water for Joe. "I haven't had much to eat today," he explained. I have a few things to say.""

"First, I'm pissed. That might seem strange as I hardly know you, but I'm pissed for you and at you. In case you hadn't wondered, I won't be flattering you with any flowery speeches today. You and your so-called friends have your collective heads up your asses. You seem to have lost all perspective. Since I may be the first person you've encountered with clean hands, because I have no stake in the matter, I think you should listen. You ready?"

Joe looked up briefly, then down in acquiescence.

"If you have something to say, say it. Because otherwise, I'm going to lay some wisdom on you."

Hearing no further reply, Andre began.

"Frankly, I'm not that impressed with you, and even less so with your friends. You all take yourselves way too seriously."

"You think your little company was going to save the world? Hardly. Now, I'm not saying you shouldn't do what is right or work on technologies to make things better. I'm as concerned about global warming as the next guy. But one person isn't going to solve it. If other companies make the panels now, and they make them cheaper, that's likely to mean faster adoption, and that's a good thing. Sucks for you and your company, I know, but likely good for the environment."

"Now, when it comes to your charities, yeah, it sucks for a foundation to go under, especially if it was doing good things. But, there are thousands of charitable foundations in this country. Do what you can, but no one of them was going to save the world. You can't put all that on yourself, nor should your friends depend on you like they seem to. They need to stand on their own two feet, stop expecting you to take care of them."

"Losing a kid has to be the worst thing in the world. I have one myself." With this, Andre pulled out his phone and showed Joe a photo, a toddler who looked little like Andre except for the adoring way he stared at his father's face, his cheek being kissed with adoration. Joe's stomach began to roil, and he turned away. "My wife is pregnant now with our second. People sometimes ask me, would you like to have a girl this time? It's a ridiculous question. I'd like to have a healthy, happy baby. We put too much on sex, or any number of other things. I love my son with everything in me and I can't imagine losing him. But—" he grabbed Joe's face again and pulled it up so that their eyes met. "But, if I ever lost him, I can't imagine abandoning Tina—that's my wife—and letting her go through things alone. No matter the circumstances, no matter what stupid thing she said. Hell, I say a dozen stupid things a day. That woman has been loyal to you; it's time to show some of that back. You think she's not hurting too? You think she feels any less pain than you do? She was driving and even though you know the crash wasn't her fault, she must feel responsible. To do anything other than to hug her and tell her she's loved, it's just unconscionable."

"The world is a lot bigger than you or your friends, your little company, your little good works, your little family that you love. I think you need to go out and experience some of that."

"My dad used to take us deep sea fishing every summer, out in his own little boat. We'd get so far from the shore, I didn't know how he found his way back, though he always did. You couldn't see anything but water and the clouds in the sky. Clouds bigger than you can imagine, like white pillows against a sky so blue you can't categorize it." Andre paused, in awe of his own memory. "The thing is, when you're out there, that far out, you realize how small you are. How little anything you do matters. One time, it started to rain, and I thought I'd be scared. It was getting dark, and we could die out there. But the same world that brings those drops of rain, brought us the fish my dad caught, it was one of our most productive days. And my dad knew his way back, regardless of the weather. And that rain, we need it, for every crop you can imagine, none of us can eat without it."

"When I say what you do doesn't matter, I don't mean don't do it. Make your life as good as it can be. Go find your Sophia. See what's happening with the pregnancy. Your son is no longer with you, but trust that you gave him a good life while he was here. Give the baby one too if you can. Grieve, of course, but the world won't revolve around your grief. It will go on and it won't give a shit whether you're a part of it or not. Make your contribution, good or bad, to your family, to the world. Remember how small you are in the grand scheme of things, and how immense you are to those small number of people who depend on you. You may not save the world, but for them, you are their world. How dare you take that world away from them?"

"You got yourself thinking you were a mighty man, a puppet master, pulling the strings of the rest of us, making the world the kind of place you envision. And somehow, your friends seem to have bought into the same idea, depending on you, either to realize your dreams, or make theirs for them. For all I know, your vision may be wonderful, but it's a tiny piece of what the world is, what it can be. How arrogant, how vain can you get? The mighty fall, always, and the world goes on. The vain get ignored, as they should. Whatever beauty, love, and amazingness there is on this planet, you can't imagine a smidgeon of it. Why did you ever think you could? None of us can. You may be smarter than most, but you don't know anything. Nothing at all."

Joe didn't look up. Couldn't. "What do I do?" he whispered.

"I have no clue. All I can tell you is what my dad told me that day on the ocean. When I didn't know how we'd get back. The world doesn't revolve around you, but it does spin. It will keep spinning long after you're gone, back to dust and ashes. I can't tell you how to find meaning when you've lost it. Not any more than I could find my way back from that ocean in the rain. What I can say is, the answer isn't wandering the streets of this city. It's not in this gym, slamming weights around. It's certainly not in some lonely hotel room."

"Where is it?" Joe's whisper was more desperate than curious.

"It's out in that ocean."

Joe's eyes were incredulous, but he still couldn't look up. Andre stood, placing a firm, but gentle hand on Joe's shoulder. "Get lost, Joe. Go someplace where you feel as small as I did that day in the ocean. You need to get lost." And with that, he walked away and returned to his work.

CHAPTER 18

Sophia exhaled a deep sigh as she pulled into the garage. Shopping was tiring enough; shopping alone while heavily pregnant was exhausting.

She popped open the trunk and looked over the supplies. She now had most of the things a new baby would need. Inexplicably, the insurance company had returned the toddler seat from her totaled car, while advising her not to use it. She'd hardly been able to look at it and cried bitterly while dumping it into the trash bin.

She now pulled a newborn car seat out of the trunk and buckled it into the back seat, facing to the rear. Experience doing so wasn't so distant that she was out of practice. Closing the door, she took two trips toting shopping bags from the trunk into the nursery. The doctor said that her due date was two weeks sooner than previously thought. She needed to be prepared for when the baby, and her husband, arrived, in whatever order.

For now, she placed her bags down inside the already-assembled crib. She emptied each systematically, first receiving blankets, into the bottom drawer, then cloth diapers, into the top drawer. In between, there were several onesies, each of them cute as can be, and five sets of baby pajamas, four of them of the feety kind, just one with open cuffs.

Tediously, she began the process of removing the toys that were too advanced for a newborn. She was thankful that Olly, the stuffed Ox, with the missing eye and the ear perpetually wet from toddler saliva, had been disposed of with the car and her son's other belongings. She didn't think she could have stood to throw him away herself, nor to have kept him.

She stumbled over the lettered blocks and decided to remove those as well. Most were in the bin within a few seconds, the remaining seven, those stacked vertically spelling out her son's name, she saved for last, and removed one at a time, stacking them upside down among the others, then mixing them together so she could no longer tell which they had been.

She had texted Joe from the store, first with questions about clothing and toy choices, then with information on which purchases she had made, all in a breezy tone that assumed he was out on an errand, ever the busy executive, not the wayward spouse. She had received no response, but remained sure that he'd be home on time. He was too good a man, too good a father, to do otherwise. Until now, he'd never missed a doctor's appointment, with either pregnancy. It was he who had rocked their son to sleep when he had colic, distracted him with stories when he was teething, and taught him songs from his own childhood, along with some he invented.

Still, his recent editorials had been painful to read. It seemed he was communicating with everyone but her, responding to nonsense chatter that had little to do with their lives, their future, their happiness. He was clearly in pain. They had been through many things together, she hoped only that they could lean on each other during this time. It seemed she would have to wait until he was ready

to lean, and to be leaned on.

She needed to be near him and knew she would again soon. It was

only a matter of time. For now, as if to maintain the connection, she

pulled her pillow and blankets off of their marital bed and took them

into the nursery. She opened the window and stared out for a

moment at the summer moon. "I'm here, Joe," she whispered.

Sleeping on the floor would be painful at this stage, but she could

manage. Sophia lay down, eyes on the open window as the breeze

blew through the room, her hand grasping the rail of the crib. She

closed her eyes, squeezed out one more tear, and drifted off to sleep.

CHAPTER 19

The ocean might have worked for that personal trainer, but though it was only a few miles away, it wasn't where Joe headed. He pulled his rental car out on the freeway and headed south. He didn't have much idea where he was going and didn't care. He just had to travel, to move, and in his weakened state, he was no longer able to do much walking around town. Besides, he felt like he'd seen it all.

He carried little in the car. His laptop remained in the hotel room, along with his suitcase. He hadn't bothered to check out. He'd brought his wallet only because he needed his credit card to rent the car. His mind was a haze. He had to wipe his eyes often just to be able to see enough to stay on the road.

Get lost was the advice, but he was driving toward familiar territory. Tulare was home, though he had few friends and family left there. The South Bay had become his life and until recently, it had not occurred to him to have regrets. Billy remained his closest connection to the valley, having tagged along as he made his fortune. Now, his friend would have to find his own way. Joe refused to think about it.

South gave way to east as the Pacheco Pass highway rose and fell quickly. He ignored the strutting peacocks at the side of the Casa de Fruta exit, neither fruit nor respite holding any appeal. He pressed the pedal, speeding toward nowhere and was soon descending the highway at a speed that would often have attracted the attention of the highway patrol. He did not note their absence.

The stretch of highway after the mountains remained boring, and was more frustrating than it had been in years past, Los Baños traffic lights held up his progress; though he had no idea where he was going, he still was in a hurry. Getting nowhere seemed more crucial than any destination he'd ever purposely targeted.

His anxiety increased as his mind grappled with what came next, a topic he'd been avoiding for weeks. Getting back to the valley was easy, what to do when he arrived there remained a mystery. He had no idea and as the landscape became more familiar, his muscles tightened.

Route 152 merged south onto Highway 99, taking Joe toward his childhood home, though he was scarcely aware of it. Joe felt his heart rate increase, his hands gripped the wheel so tightly, his knuckles ached, then cracked. He had to get off this path, off this road. Home was nowhere, held nothing for him.

Going back wasn't an option either; there was nothing at that home either. He felt as homeless as he'd been perceived walking the streets with no place to go. South toward childhood, north toward his recent past, neither led anywhere. Suddenly, he took the first exit he saw, Highway 145, though he didn't see the sign. His drive was now random.

Drops began falling on his windshield, not a fine mist, but large ones plopping down hard before his eyes. He didn't turn the wipers on and within a minute, the rain was pouring, limiting his visibility. He turned randomly, the new highway trending northeast now, signs he passed, but didn't register, gave the mileage to Yosemite. He barely kept the car in the lane, horns blared as other drivers avoided collision. Towns passed by, Coursegold, Oakhurst, then gave way to campgrounds. He'd brought no equipment, no tent, no sleeping bag, much less a reservation for this popular tourist destination. He travelled on, traffic thinning, then a warning light flashed on the dashboard display. He ignored it and persisted north, still away from San Jose, the road veering east again.

Half Dome came within sight, but the rain cloaked all, coming down heavily enough to obscure anything outside the car. Joe had only intermittent glimpses of landmarks; the lines on the road barely visible.

Something beeped on the dashboard, then beeped again persistently. The car began sputtering. Finally, it came to a stop, in the center of the roadway, blocking traffic in both directions. Joe fumbled with his seat belt, released the clasp, and clambered out and into the woods.

Running, panting, his heart racing, he pushed on. Away from the road, away from anything reeking of technology, of the familiar, of a life or a world known and disillusioning. Joe stumbled, fell into the mud, then fell again. He slowed out of necessity, looked around.

The rain poured, dripping from his chin, his sleeves, his fingertips. He paused, looked every direction, knowing nothing of which was each. His gazed up, the clouds obscuring the stars, trees swaying in the wind. There were no landmarks now, even had he had the knowledge to read them.

He had done all he could to avoid a destination. Joe was now very much lost.

CHAPTER 20

The rain was mild in San Jose and the morning light shone through the window blinds as Angel opened them. Her smile was beatific as she quietly went about her life of service. It wasn't clear who would be in the conference room today, if anyone, but she wanted to be prepared. She made coffee, regular and decaf, and she had pastries available. The CEO was missing, the CFO had resigned, but she was confident beyond the evidence of things she could see.

She turned the monitors on, each financial channel providing similar perspectives on the same news. Commodity prices were up, but pundits advised caution. Tech stocks were down, but the financial advisors were annoyingly enthusiastic on one channel, apocalyptic on another. She turned the volume down low; words were unnecessary.

The suite of offices and cubicles outside were quiet. Most of the staff had left, assuming layoffs that hadn't officially come. The company wouldn't be able to make payroll much longer, they were sure, so what was the point?

She set folders out on the table, twelve of them, one at each setting, though she knew not all those seats would be filled. She hadn't seen half of the chairs occupied in weeks, but she went about her routine as she always had.

Just as Angel was preparing to leave the room, she heard the words on one of the channels, "and news from yesterday's trade discussions..." She turned the volume up on that channel, muting the others.

"As we reported yesterday, the US/China trade talks have reached their conclusion. Previous reports of changes in tariff practices have proved to be erroneous. China has dropped demands for that concession in exchange for the opening of US markets in other areas. For more on how this impacts the US industries, we go now to..."

Angel continued with her work, placing a pen and folder with today's agenda at each place setting. She glanced quickly at the ticker on the screen and Solar Champions stock was already up to $8.53 per share and climbing. Once she had watered the creeping fig plants, it was up to $12.42, when finished with the grape ivy, it was over $15. With quiet resolve, she exited the prepared conference room and began knocking on the doors of various executives, inviting them down the hall. By the time she finished her rounds, ten seats were filled, four men, six women, all at rapt attention. The stock price had already climbed to $47.89, and pundits were expecting it to go higher. CNBC was promoting last fall's documentary on Joe, with a follow-up segment on the Joe and Sophia Taylor Foundation, with a number at the bottom of the screen for people to donate.

Angel walked over to the corner of the room and checked the coffee levels. Both urns were still half filled. She looked around the room, examined the dumbfounded expressions on the various vice presidents, chairs, and other executives, and pondered for a moment how long it would take for them to realize that they were the ones who were called upon now, those who needed to take action. It didn't matter; they'd figure it out eventually.

Her work complete, Angel walked out of the room, unnoticed, carrying nothing but her watering can. Laughing to herself, she opened the window facing east, pulled aside the branches and poured water on the fig tree below. Leaving the window open, she swept over to the west side and did the same with the lilies on the sill. She paused for a moment, allowing the cross breeze to mix the contrasting scents. Heavenly, she told herself.

Angel paused, taking several deep breaths, then looked down into the water canister, considered refilling it for later, but it remained more than half full. She replaced it in its usual spot on the counter, then gazed across the room to the east. As the morning sun broke through the descending raindrops, she was sure that just past the city skyline, a rainbow was forming.

CHAPTER 21

In the paradise of California, fires raged. Thick underbrush kindled with a heat rarely seen, smoke from pine needles rose, along with ashes and the occasional spark, setting trees aflame, mid-trunk, squirrels and chipmunks roasted when they could not flee. The wind carried the detritus far and wide, ash scattering on cars parked on freeways far from the flames.

Animals sought safer ground where they could, perished when they could not. Bears travelled to lower ground, interacting with locals and scaring tourists. Some were captured in photos and shared among family and friends; others were captured by bullets fired by those who saw the picturesque rural areas as theirs and bears as interlopers.

The ground cracked after years of drought. Structures weakened, overpasses and bridges became shaky, a few collapsing, others remaining, public confidence waning. Graffiti shifted as if by an earthquake, patterns disrupted by the shifting of concrete several inches. Taller buildings swayed in the wind.

From the west, the storms came, a series of them. The wind that had been spreading ash now spread a mixture of ash and water, a muck that congealed on cars, mailboxes, and rooftops. In the mountains, as the fires cooled, the muck slid down hills, uprooting centuries-old trees, and boulders that had lain in place for millennia. Rivers and streams were rerouted in an instant, the wildlife depending on them moving on or becoming prey.

The fire and rain intertwined, the sunny days people thought would not end, did in fact end, and were replaced with weeks with the sun beyond sight, such that many thought it was in fact the rainy days that would not end. Memories are short.

Freeways came to a standstill, whole lanes washed away, crashes putting emergency services to the test. Landslides created new lanes down mountainsides, whole groves washed out in an instant, seedlings planted randomly for new ones, far from their original location. The concept of native plants became stretched as the wind bore spores from farther away. What was considered natural or normal was disrupted, and new definitions created, to be themselves washed away in less than a generation. The necessity of adaptability was proved yet again, then as quickly forgotten.

Fires sparked by humans were quickly extinguished in the floods and just as quickly, new ones ignited, from lightning, from overturned technology of various origins, from seemingly spontaneous sources. The new fires undermined infrastructure yet further, straining resources and redefining the definition of emergency. Otherwise important medical calls went unanswered as priorities narrowed.

Among animal species, humans included, responses varied. Some hunkered and were either washed away or burned; others did the same and their refuge became a sanctuary while they built resilience for a new start. Others travelled far, escaping the madness or being pulled into it, swirling, twisting until their orientation to time and place was lost. Adaptability was proven the highest test, though one riven with randomness and unpredictability. Several species were lost, and a few nascent ones took their places, planting themselves in loose and loosening soil in the unconscious hope that whatever actions they took, whether from instinct or strategy, might prove the lucky one.

In the south, traffic and work stalled, human productivity reaching a generational nadir. On the coast, technology grappled and failed. In the north, dams burst, cracked, or were overrun. In the valley and mountains between, all of these came to a head, combating and interlacing at once. Natural and supernatural forces were on supreme display, for all observers to witness, feel, and absorb, though not at all to understand.

What was least clear, to those who attempted to observe, was whether these forces were competing or conspiring. Or whether it in fact even mattered.

CHAPTER 22

Joe stood, stumbled on through the underbrush. His jeans were ripped, and more than once, the tatters tangled themselves in manzanita and other bushes. He ripped free, then pulled apart the bottoms of each leg.

The clouds had blocked out the sky all afternoon, but now, evening approached, or so it seemed. Darkness prevailed. He had to find a path somewhere. In one of the most popular national parks in the world, surely, one wouldn't be far.

Rivulets trickled down the hills as Joe climbed, soaking his shoes with mud. Two steps up, half a step sliding back down.

Ash from the wildfires was being blown in the wind, swirling with the rain. Joe could taste it on his tongue each time a drop fell. He followed one of the streams to a newly formed gully at the top of a ridge. The scars on his back ached, and burned from the ash droppings. A ponderosa cone fell from a nearby tree, catching in his shirt and pulling at one of the scabs. Joe screamed in pain.

Reaching around his back, he could not grasp the cone; he had to rub against a nearby tree to knock it off. The blood dripped down his back, mixing with the rain, ash, and sap. Another cone fell, a cedar, less prickly. He wondered if he was imagining the smell.

Joe walked toward the middle of the gully, nearly waist high in mud and water, then turned slowly around. He felt his feet slip, the ridge was steeper than he'd thought. He looked back, thinking it was the direction he'd come from, but no longer sure. He slipped into the water with the faint hope that he would find relief. Tangles of vines pulled at the open scars, tearing them. He allowed his head to drop below the surface, then opened his eyes. Several rainbow trout swam by, showing no curiosity toward their invader. Joe sat up quickly, then stood as the water was coming down so fast that soon he wouldn't be able to breathe seated. He looked across the divide, saw only another ridge in the distance, then another.

Joe screamed again, his indictment resounding across the hills. He screamed another time. Flora and fauna ignored him, perhaps pointedly, mockingly.

A flash blinded his eyes from a distance, then a loud crack. Lightning and thunder, remarkably close together. A jagged bolt struck not a mile away. Joe thought a fire may have ignited, but if so, the rain doused it. The elements seemed to be competing with one another.

Joe screamed again, his despair existential as much as physical. Scars broke open down his back, but he no longer noticed. His scream rang out again, buried in the whirling rain. His throat was raw from lack of fluid intake, and his own guttural rumblings. He screamed again and no one heard, not a creature turned its head. Joe fell backwards against the bank, his knees buckling. He closed his eyes and heard another crack.

The flashes were spreading across the sky when he opened his eyes. A two-hundred-foot-tall fir tree split down the middle, each half falling, not to the ground, but leaning against neighboring trees, creaking as the weight bore down.

In the new gap in the forest, stars were visible. The trees swayed, but between them, he recognized Pleiades, the Seven Sisters, each glimmering with a distinct effervescence. He searched the stars, seeking a message he could comprehend, and received only the glow, bright and luminous.

Joe sank to his knees, his energy spent. The rain paused, but for the first time, he was cold. He trembled violently, shivers coursing through his body in waves. His brain convulsed, driving thought away. His eyes blurred, senses distorted.

A branch broke behind him, then another. Before Joe could look, the mud pulled him down, the gully, washed away, taking Joe with it. He slid down the hill and tumbled to the rocks below.

CHAPTER 23

Sophia carefully parked her Prius on the second floor of the hospital parking garage. Her midwife had already warned her that they may want her to stay over a second night if Joe wasn't here to drive her home. He wasn't. This wasn't the plan, but she would exercise patience. The baby was coming whether she was ready or not, and regardless of where its father might be, or in what state of mind.

The contractions were coming closer now, just three or four minutes apart. Traffic had been heavier than expected and she should have remembered that second babies come faster than the first. Her bag had been ready for weeks, and she just managed to make it through the doors of the maternity ward before doubling

over. A nurse came over quickly and asked her name. "My name is

Chaz," he said, though Sophia barely heard. "I understand you've

been through this before?"

"Yes," she replied between ragged breaths. "Once."

"Well, then I'm sure things will go great. I'm just starting my shift,

so I'll be seeing you through your labor, and, if I am guessing

correctly, the birth of your little one before the night is over."

Sophia nodded, mildly reassured.

Two hours later, she was pushing. Chaz was holding her hand, the

midwife in the catcher's seat, ready to take hold of the incoming

infant. "OK hon," Chaz encouraged. "Ready for another big push?"

Sophia closed her eyes, then looked up at Chaz, nodding. "Let's

go." Only in her mind did she whisper, *Get here soon Joe.*

A scream shattered her reverie. She couldn't remember the last

push. The baby was here, crying as though its world had been turned

inside out. She tried to look down, between her knees.

"A girl," the midwife said. "You have a beautiful, healthy little girl here."

"You did great," Chaz told her. Sophia nodded in gratitude.

"May I see her?"

"In just a moment. Just a little cleanup and we'll have her right here with you. We know family time is important."

Now, Chaz was placing the baby on her torso. "I understand you intend to breastfeed?"

She was lifting her daughter to her breast. It took a few moments, but soon, she latched on.

Chaz looked on. "I see you don't have much more need of me. Before I go, this doesn't have to be decided now, but, have you and your husband picked out a name?"

"My mother."

"Pardon?"

"She's going to be named after my mother," Sophia replied, beaming. "Her name is Faith."

"Of course," Chaz replied, smiling. I'll get the forms. With that, he stepped out of the room, leaving mother and child to bond. His job was   done.

CHAPTER 24

The dawn sun pierced his eyelids from between the fir trees. Joe woke with a start, cold water washing over his back. Moss had accumulated among his scars, tangling in them. He looked up and found the reflection from the snowcaps blinding in its silent beauty. As the stream washed around him, jagged rocks cut into his legs. He pulled himself slowly to his feet, not knowing if the pains in his legs were from sleep or injury.

Joe looked around. The weather had cleared, at least momentarily. On the western ridge, if he could get to it, there were small patches of dry ground. He reached for a walking stick, but the wet, green branch only bent too easily, providing no support. He tried another, but it snapped. Finally, he used his hands and elbows to climb, grasping the extended twigs and vines, hoping they wouldn't slip out of the damp earth as he sought footholds. More than once, he slipped down, losing ground, but he continued, not sure where he was going, just knowing that higher must be better, or at least, drier.

The ridge was an overhang now, jutting out over Joe, but not enough to provide shade, the sun heated his back, sweat dripping, making it harder to grasp things. Animals, trapped in burrows through days of rain, now peered out, ducking back in their holes as Joe ascended.

As he neared the top, he grasped a handhold, half warm dirt, half rock, looking for the next, when something slithered across his fingertips. A familiar rattle, and he whipped his head around.

The diamond-shaped one peered at him, and hissed. One warning rattle was all he was likely to receive; he needed to pull back quickly, but handholds were few in number, and slippery. Another hiss, and Joe withdrew, dangling now from his left hand, the rattler barely within view.

When the hawk swooped down, he almost lost his remaining grip, its wings brushed Joe's face as it pulled the reptile from its burrow and flew off. It was the snake that was now dangling, helplessly snapping, predator having become prey in an instant.

Joe found a new foothold, summoned his remaining strength, and gained the top of the ridge in several ponderous steps. He paused, considered resting, but fearing he would not be able to move if he stopped, walked on. The sun was again behind slate-gray clouds, the air acrid and humid, mist beginning to turn into another light drizzle.

There was no path. Wet and dry segments of the woods alternated. Joe plodded on, emaciated, and exhausted. He began to wonder if he was hallucinating. He was seeing animals, first those you'd expect to come out after the rain; deer, squirrels, and chipmunks. But later, mules and goats. He wondered if the Park Service used them as pack animals. Every few steps, he thought he caught voices, but each time he stopped, it seemed to have been the wind. More than once, he thought he spied a family on the opposite side. As he turned to warn them of the treacherous terrain, they disappeared. Surely, it was a mirage.

The rain slid down the overhang like thick sheets of paper, and Joe began looking for shelter. Small depressions in the rock were all he found. The first provided nothing as the rain slipped in, washing down his face and neck. Rounding a corner, he found another, but it was occupied. He had not imagined the goats; this one bleated at him. Joe prepared to retreat, and just as he turned, the goat leaped past, bleating once more in exasperation. Joe slipped into the space between the rocks.

Ducking inside, Joe found that the water came from everywhere, above, dripping on his head, and building around his feet. The dirt turned to a viscous mud. He tried to bury his face between rocks, but found no hiding place there. Where the rain didn't try to drown him, jagged stones and branches poked at his nose and ears. Each time he moved, another body part was cut or bruised. His feet slipped again and again, and with nothing to grasp, Joe realized that he would need to leave this non-shelter.

He rounded the corner again, into the open downpour. Across the way, another dark depression in the rock wall appeared. He clambered toward it, alternating between grasping vines and nothing at all, sure that at any moment he would slide down into the creek that was closer to a river now.

Thirty feet turned to twenty, then ten. His hands were bloody, but he found the spot; it was more than a depression. It was nearly a tunnel. At the least, a small cave, a space to dry off and hide from the storm.

Joe realized he had walked at least fifteen feet into the cave and the only water drops he felt were those coming down his hands and face. The sky was a tiny oasis coming through a winding series of crags above.

Joe slid to the ground. He found that he had a view of the rushing water below. The wind circulated through the tunnels above and the water raging downstream. he was caught between, in a whirlwind of sound. He heard voices. He could not make out words, but in the cacophony, his friends seemed present, Ellie, Billy, Zaida, arguing perhaps. But they drifted as if washing downstream with the rain.

Then, came the quiet, calm voice of Angel Ortiz. Was it her? He couldn't be sure. All he knew was the whirlwind, dark and swirling. Whether Angel's voice, or perhaps just the wind, the small, still whisper filled his mind and lulled Joe into a fitful slumber.

All night, whirling through the cave, the wind continued to speak.

CHAPTER 25

The door to Ellie's office opened and Billy walked in. Ellie cradled the phone to her chin and waved him over to the chair in front of her. She finished up with her call, making notes in her pad in front of her, hung up and turned to Billy. "How have you been?"

"Good, good, of course. Heard from Joe?"

"Right to the point. No, I haven't. You?"

"No, not in a while."

"I didn't think so. It's a sad situation, but frankly, not why I invited you here. I understand you were involved in Joe's foundation?"

"Yes, I used to be."

"I know, the foundation is in an unusual place right now. Hard to say whether it will survive. I'm told the lawsuits have been settled for a smaller amount than previously expected. It seems those workers really believed in what they were doing."

"We all believed."

"I assume you still do, right? I mean, the foundation and its work weren't about a cult of personality. It was about the good works. At least, I'd like to think so."

"Of course, it was."

"Good. That's what I thought. The organization may never be what it was. We don't know if or when Joe will return and Sophia has other matters to deal with." Ellie let out a sigh, then continued. "You see, the work we do here through the church was affected as well. Our homeless outreach. Our youth programs."

"I didn't know."

"You wouldn't. That's because these didn't go through the foundation at all. Joe and Sophia weren't ones to put all their eggs in one basket, not in investing, and not in their charitable work. But their largesse is a big part of what made us successful, what helped us have an impact on our community. And Billy, we were really changing things."

"What does that have to do with me? I'm not very religious."

"You don't need to be for what I have in mind." Ellie grabbed a newspaper article she'd placed to the side of her desk and a few other papers. "You see, Joe had more impact than he realized. He inspired people, not just with his money or the things he did with it, but just by who he was. I'm told he wrote a letter to some obscure publication neither of us has likely every heard of. It went a bit viral."

"What does that mean?"

"I'm not sure yet. For the Joe and Sophia Taylor Foundation, it may mean that their problems aren't as bad as they thought. Donations poured in and most of their debts have been paid off. Insurance covered the settlements, and the land is still there. Apparently, the letter led to a lot of other organizations getting donations as well, big ones from other corporate leaders, and thousands of small ones. They're still coming in. Joe and Sophia may not be able to lead anymore, but the work still needs to be done, right?"

"Of course, but who's going to do it?"

"Who indeed?" Ellie looked at him for a moment, waiting.

"What? You can't mean?"

"You worked on the music education program right? Played and taught in the schools?"

"Not really. Mostly, I coordinated. I mean, I haven't played in..."

"So, you coordinated. That makes you a leader."

"I've never thought of myself that way."

"How we think of ourselves can change, Billy. I'm a pastor, so I guess that makes me a leader too." She paused again. "Look, the work you did was important, right?"

"Yes, but..."

"So, the importance of it didn't change because Joe isn't here. If anything, it just means new people need to step up."

"You and I?"

"It's a start. The music education program and our outreach efforts were separate, but they're all part of the same thing, aren't they? Helping people create a better world and make sense of it."

"I've never thought of it in quite those terms."

"Yeah, that might be a bit grandiose. But we relieved suffering when we could. And music puts beauty in the world, if anything does.

174

All I mean is, there's no reason the work can't continue. And no reason we can't make sure it does."

Billy pondered for a moment. "I could still do the music, and I'd be happy to work on that with homeless and church kids as well as youth in schools. But, I know nothing of structure, organization, much less fundraising. Joe handled all of that. I'm not really an organization guy. I just like to do the work."

"I see. I know a bit about organization, having led this church for fifteen years. It's a smaller scale of course. I don't know law, bureaucracy, and well, I haven't had to fundraise for a while." She paused for a moment. "Wait, I know just who can help."

Zaida was still driving east, somewhere near Ohio, when the call came in. She took it through the car's speakers and tried for several minutes to keep up with the enthusiasm she was hearing from the other end as Ellie and Billy talked over each other outlining their plans and dreams.

She pulled to the side of the road and drew her notepad and pen from her purse. She looked up at the sky as a shaft of light pierced the windshield. When there was finally a pause, she spoke up. "OK, I think I understand now. How can I help?"

Billy arrived back at his apartment late in the evening, exhilarated. His hands trembled as he opened the door and put his things down. He had a folder of notes outlining their all-day discussion and a task list more than two pages long. He would do it all, and more, but not today.

He picked up an apple from a bowl on the counter and ate it while sorting through the mail, along with a generous cup of milk. When finished, he walked over, resolutely, to the closet, pulled out the long black case, and opened it. Surprisingly, his hands didn't tremble as he pulled the instrument out. He closed his eyes and took thirty seconds of deep, fulfilling breaths. Then, he moistened and pursed his lips and blew. The long, sonorous notes of his trombone filled the neighborhood and fed the souls of all within earshot.

CHAPTER 26

For the second morning, Joe awoke to the sounds of nature, and dazzling shafts of light entering the cave horizontally through gaps in the walls.

It wasn't the light that alerted him this time, but rather a raspy tongue licking his face, warm breath accompanying it. Another tongue soothed the sores on his back. His thoughts turned to stray dogs, reminiscent of his time spent wandering the streets. He shoved away the closest wet nose, ignoring the grunts and growls that greeted him. He turned, prepared to shoo away the other creature as well, when the next growl he heard was deeper, menacing.

Joe's eyes opened with a start. Two small bear cubs looked up at him, one pawing at his hand as if to play. Joe barely noticed them, his eyes fixed on their mother, standing on her hind legs, her ominous voice reverberating through the cave. Joe backed away, looking for his things before realizing he carried none. The mama bear approached, and Joe continued to retreat, exiting where he had entered the previous day. Looking down, he saw water raging. What he remembered as a stream yesterday, a simple tributary, was now a river. Jumping was not an option.

Neither was going back the way he had come. As the bear approached, her cubs seemed to taunt him from her heels. Joe headed upward. Fear proved a great motivator, so the footholds seemed to be plentiful as Joe climbed higher and higher, unsure of his next steps. He slipped several times, but always caught himself.

Behind him, the bear gave him a long, final warning roar, making it clear that Joe's trip should be a one-way journey. He took the hint with enthusiasm.

As he climbed further, the path finally widened. He no longer needed to crawl on hands and knees. The rain was a long, slow drizzle, washing the blood and mud down his arms and legs. His shirt was mostly gone, his pants in tatters. Joe's face was raw. His body was stripped of all adornment, the wounds scarred over. He was thinner than he'd ever been.

Joe was the solitary human within miles. One of the biggest tourist destinations in the world was abandoned. Nature had been upended. No creatures stirred. Ash from the wildfires swirled but was batted down by the silent rain. Trees had fallen. Where there had been paths, they were no longer visible. Joe stumbled backward over a sign, breaking it in two. Had he stopped to look, he'd have seen the arrow pointing with the designation Illiloeutte Falls.

Plodding further, Joe came across a fallen pine, its wide trunk exposed. Bark beetles swarmed and fed on the decay. Water ran down the sides, but the vast width of the tree provided shelter; underneath, the ground was nearly dry. Joe looked up at the mid-day sun. One final time he opened his mouth, emitting a silent scream.

His knees collapsed and Joe knelt, prostrate among the dust and ashes, at last giving himself over completely. Nothing entered or left his body or mind except breath, slow and deep.

Then, the wave came.

Joe did not look up. He did not open his eyes. He let the water take him. He rode it down, spiraling, twisting, until it laid him gently on the surface of the Merced River. On his back, eyes closed, he rode through the rainstorm, into the valley sun, on toward his Sophia, his Faith, what remained and whatever shall be.

ACKNOWLEDGMENTS

I have read many sources about the book of Job, from Carl Jung to William Blake, to Robert Heinlein. Academic writers have chimed in, each with their take, all of them different as the text is one of the most mysterious out there.

So I had to add my own voice to the cacophony, for whatever it might be worth. Perhaps I'd heard too many people refer to "the patience of Job." I wondered if they hadn't read past the first two chapters. In my view, this is not a story of patience at all.

I had the original ideas for this take a few years ago, the marriage of Job and the modern world. I knew the place in the world Joe would have and I had some idea how the story would end.

But it was through conversations with my friend Ann Marie Wagstaff, who knows the Bible better than anyone I know, that I came to better understand the structure of the text and how to make this work, if indeed it does. So, I am indebted to her in this, as in many things.

My writers group provided key advice, even when they were unsure of what I was doing, so thanks also to Ann Marie, Cheryl Porter, Neal Blakie, and Aerin Ridgeway.

Thank you also for Laurie Buchholz who read the text in an early stage and provided comments. If I knew how to take your suggestion to turn it into a screenplay, I'd give it a shot. Maybe someday. Melissa Long was invaluable in editing and raising important questions I hadn't considered.

To Lucas, who inspires me daily to make something more of this world than what it is. And Rebecca Baird who fed the dying embers in me. I don't know the source of the fuel we're burning, but I've learned not to question it.

ABOUT THE AUTHOR

Michael Carley is a writer, among a few other things, from central California. His non-fiction work has appeared in the web-zine No Depression, The Good Men Project, and The Andrew Goodman Foundation web site. He penned a weekly column for the *Porterville Recorder* from 2010 to 2019. His first novel, *Know My Name*, was published in 2016 and his novella *People Like That* in 2020. In 2022, his memoir, *Diary of a Bad Husband* was published. Mr. Carley lives in Porterville California with his son.